Praise for "Judas Kiss"

"Fox has crafted a tense and twisty urban fantasy packed with action and a touch of mystery. JUDAS KISS is one Hells of a ride!"
—Danielle Harrington,
Author of *The Diseased Ones*

Praise for "The Devil's Own"

"THE DEVIL'S OWN is an unstoppable story that hooks you right from the start. This spellbinding debut will make K.A. Fox one of your new favorite authors. A must read for all lovers of dark fantasy."
—Jessica Therrien,
Best-selling author of *Children of the Gods*

"THE DEVIL'S OWN is an exciting work of young adult urban fantasy. A superb novel for teen horror and urban fantasy enthusiasts."
—Readers Favorite,
5 Star Review

For my family, who never doubted.

MURPHY'S LAW: BOOK TWO

JUDAS KISS

K.A. FOX

FBI Anti-Piracy Warning: The unauthorized reproduction or distribution of a copyrighted work is illegal. Criminal copyright infringement, including infringement without monetary gain, is investigated by the FBI and is punishable by up to five years in federal prison and a fine of $250,000.

Advertencia Antipirateria del FBI: La reproducción o distribución no autorizada de una obra protegida por derechos de autor es ilegal. La infracción criminal de los derechos de autor, incluyendo la infracción sin lucro monetario, es investigada por el FBI y es castigable con pena de hasta cinco años en prisión federal y una multa de $250,000.

Judas Kiss
First Edition
Copyright © 2020 K.A. Fox
All rights reserved. No part of this book may be used or reproduced in any manner whatsoever, including Internet usage, without written permission from the author.

This story is a work of fiction. References to real people, events, establishments, organizations, or locales are intended only to provide a sense of authenticity and are used fictitiously. All other characters, and all incidents and dialogue are drawn from the author's imagination and are not to be construed as real.

Book interior designed and formatted by Debra Cranfield Kennedy.

www.acornpublishingllc.com

ISBN—Hardcover 978-1-947392-78-6
ISBN—Paperback 978-1-947392-77-9

Chapter One

THE HAND IN my hair was cruel, yanking on the sweat-soaked strands while shoving my face toward a collision with the cold wall in front of me. I gasped, resisting the forward momentum working against me, but the force was too strong. I sucked in a breath and prepared myself for the coming impact. This was going to hurt.

At the last moment, the wavering sheen of a shield popped into place between my nose and the rough bricks. It stopped me short, the ache resonating through my teeth nothing at all compared to what might have been. The fingers tangled in my mahogany curls released, setting me free. I turned to face my attacker.

"How many times do we have to do this before you remember to use your magic while you're fighting?" Callum spit the words at me in frustration. "It's a simple shield spell, Delaney. You've been able to do that for years. Do you actually want me to hurt you?"

I didn't say anything, wary as I circled my way around him. It was Cal's job to teach me everything he knew about fighting, something he was very good at. In the past weeks, I'd learned more than I'd thought I could. I'd also come to realize that he believed the best teaching was in doing, and if it left you with a few bruises to remember the lesson by, so much the better. This was a different side of him, one he hadn't shown me before. And it was my own fault. I'd made it necessary.

Keeping my eyes on him, I shook my arms out, ready for what was to come. He sighed and shook his head. "Enough for today. I can't have Angus seeing you with blood on your face. I like living too much."

Surprised, I reached up to feel for the blood, thinking I must have mistaken it for sweat. My guard relaxed and Callum flew at me, his hands a blur, diving for my midsection. I dropped back on my heels, letting my hands intercept his fist, but he used that contact to knock me off balance, his bulk winning the battle as I hit the floor, pinned by the weight of him. His fist flew toward my chin and something tore loose in my chest as I screamed. A wave of force exploded out from my core.

Cal was blown off me, skidding across the concrete basement floor until he came to a stop against the far wall. I could hear the air rush out of him from across the open space but fought the urge to go check on him. He was fine. We both were. As fine as the daughter of the devil and one of his soldiers could be.

Shaking himself as if he needed to clear his head, he crawled onto his knees and caught his breath before meeting my eyes. "Finally," he said. There was almost a hint of approval in his voice, but he covered it quickly. "Do it again."

There was no point in arguing. Cal was already on his feet and he was going to push me until my legs were noodles and I couldn't hold my arms up. Then he was going to push a little further. I clambered up, ready for him to come at me again, knowing how fast he could move when he didn't hold back.

I didn't have a second to catch my breath before he attacked again. He threw a wave of energy at me, the force of it bruising my shoulder as I dodged out of the way. He kept coming, forcing me to retreat, off balance. I planted a shield in place as one of the waves hit and it bounced off, into the bricks, leaving a gouge behind.

Still he pressed me, more waves of energy hitting. I felt my shield start to waver. If it had been glass, I'd have sworn I could hear it cracking. I maneuvered around him, trying to choose my ground, but he cut me off, hammering away. Heat pricked my skin as he added fire to his onslaught. Sweat poured from me. I chanced a look at him as I tried to find a way out. His chiseled face was pure focus, jaw clenched with effort and probably a little anger.

My shield failed and the power he'd been casting burst through, engulfing me in the wave. Heat seared me. Pain was a bright flaring fire in my nerves, but I held on as long as

I could, the force building in me with each second. When I was filled with it, stretched until I couldn't contain any more, I let it loose. The power rushed away from me with a scream, focused and direct, right into Cal's midsection. He flew backwards, bouncing as he hit the ground. Stunned.

I carefully approached him, offering him my hand as he blinked up at me. He stood slowly with my help, his gaze taking in the singed hair and raw redness of my exposed skin. I knew the words he was going to say even before they left his mouth.

"I'm sorry, Laney." I felt the truth of them hit me deep. "I went too far."

I didn't say anything, searching his eyes. I could see pain and regret swirling in them. He'd been wanting to teach me a lesson that he believed could someday save me, but the way things were between us now, his control had slipped, and his emotions won out.

I squeezed his hand in understanding, no words needed. I wasted a wish on what might have been, before I'd broken a promise and used magic to keep him safe while I put myself in danger. Damned good intentions.

I walked away, knowing our training was done for today. There was a time when he'd wanted to teach me other things. Intimate things. But that was gone. This was all I had. What I deserved.

Chapter Two

Moose, the Hell Hound I'd been gifted by my father, was sleeping in the plush gray dog bed we kept in the corner of the kitchen, near the floor vent. He loved to nap there when the heat was running. And as cold as I constantly seemed to be this time of year, the heat was almost always on. He didn't even lift his head when I dragged myself upstairs, the door creaking open as I leaned my weight against it. The steady rise and fall of his breathing was evidence he wasn't going to be disturbed by anything smaller than a major catastrophe.

Moose wasn't the only one in the kitchen. Torren was waiting for me, seated at the table. I knew he'd been lurking, feeling each blow I took and every emotion I'd fought through with Cal. The tension in his shoulders and the sparkling-clean counters told me how hard it had been for him to stay here and not intervene. The three of us training together had quickly proved impossible. When Tor felt I was at risk, he couldn't help himself. He'd stepped in front of every punch aimed for me. Cal had finally thrown his hands up and declared he would train us individually. But that didn't change anything for Torren. In fact, it made things more difficult. I knew being stuck up here and forced to wait for every round to be over was harder on him than taking the full force of the impact.

Tor got up, reaching into the fridge and handing me a protein shake he'd mixed up. With his arms folded tight across his chest, he watched me drink down every last bit. When I finished, he took the cup from me, rinsing it out and placing it carefully into the dishwasher, his movements precise and controlled.

"You okay?" he asked, no inflection in his voice. Measured and even. The same way he did each time I emerged from training beat down, looking like I'd lost the battle. Which was every day.

I gave him the same answer every time he asked. "Fine." I lied and he knew it, but we didn't talk about that. He simply accepted it because I needed him to. Swiping futilely at the sweat on my face, I ignored the bite of the salt as it leaked into a bloody scratch on my cheek. I could have cleaned myself off downstairs, but knowing Tor was up here, needing to see proof that I was all right, I chose differently. And I needed a little distance from Cal.

"You don't have to keep doing this," Torren said. He finally turned to face me, locking me in place with the pain in his eyes. "We can go somewhere. Anywhere. I'd leave with you. We can hide." There was a desperation under his words that hadn't been there before. As if he'd been fighting the desire to say this to me for a long time. He came toward me and I made myself stay where I was, to not step back. I refused to run away from him or the need I could feel radiating from his core.

He stopped and gently brushed his fingers along the back of my hand, up my arm until he reached my shoulder. His thumb moved across my cheek until it came to my lips. He leaned down, as if he would kiss me again, like the first time. The kiss that had ruined his life. I didn't want him to kiss me, but I couldn't bring myself to pull away, the connection between us too strong and I was so tired from fighting against everything swirling around us all.

Moose whined, the sound enough to break through the paralysis that had seized me. Torren's lips hovered over mine, his breath warm against my cheek. Common sense restored, I put my hand on his chest, pushing him back to create enough distance so he would have to listen to me. "Angus would find us anywhere we tried to go. And Callum is doing everything he can to prepare us for whatever we may have to fight. Running isn't the answer." He didn't step away from me like I'd hoped. Instead, he leaned into my hand, the heat of him crossing the space between us. I closed my eyes and could see the bond tying us together. It was normally gold but today there were tongues of red and orange woven through it, like liquid fire. His need flared across our connection and I gasped at the strength of it. I had to fix this, somehow.

"Torren!" Cal's voice was sharp, cutting the tension between us. "Your turn. I'll meet you downstairs. Get ready."

Tor flushed and his anger boiled into me. I swayed, catching myself as I stumbled back, knocked off balance by the sudden power of the emotion. Both men reached to help me, but I waved them away. "I'm okay." My voice was shaky, and I hated the sound of it. I stood up straight, my feet planted securely. I put my hands out, warning them away from me. "I'm fine. Really." I made my words firm, allowing no argument. We all had things to figure out. A little emotional overload couldn't interfere with the important things we had to deal with.

Torren gave me a long look but then nodded, pushing by Callum on his way downstairs to our basement training room. Cal didn't say anything, just let him go, and for that I was grateful. Cal understood Tor was in a bad place. He also knew how important it was for Torren to learn the skills he needed to survive. If he didn't, he'd die. It was that simple.

When the door to the basement had slammed, Cal turned his attention to me. Moose came to my side, his presence warm and comforting as he pressed up against my leg. "Are you sure you're okay, Laney? You looked..." He paused, choosing his words. "You looked lost for a moment."

I shook my head, wanting to deny the truth of what he

said. "It's getting worse. He's not fighting this anymore. He's not even trying. It's almost like he wants to give in to it. I'm so afraid of what that will do to him."

Cal sighed. "You can't force him into these choices. They're his to make."

"Even if they destroy him?"

His voice was sad as he answered me. "Even then."

Chapter Three

WE WRAPPED UP our day as we always did, a family dinner for the four of us. Callum and Torren usually rotated the cooking duties. I offered to cook tonight.

Cal shook his head. "You'll understand if I'm not too excited about eating something you make. After last time." He winked and shot me his crooked grin. Moose huffed, the sound suspiciously like laughter, as he rested by the table. He was always on alert when food was mentioned, ready to snatch the opportunity to steal an accidentally dropped bit of meat or even broccoli. The crazy Hound definitely had a thing for broccoli.

I teased them in return. "It was only the one time, you big babies. Hells, work a spell on a guy and your dog and they'll never let you forget it."

That pulled a laugh from Cal. "One of these days, we'll let you cook again. Under close supervision. I kinda like having free will."

Torren joined in, the humor we shared seeming to have relaxed him. "Can't say I'm sorry I missed out on that. Never thought I'd feel like a concussion was the better part of the deal."

I smiled, appreciating the amicable atmosphere we'd managed to cultivate. It might not last, but I'd enjoy every second of it, rare as it was. "So, what's for dinner then? Since I'm not allowed to cook it."

Tor held up a box of pasta. "Spaghetti. Simple and easy."

I gave him a mock groan. "Again? Don't you know how to make anything else?

He glared at me even as a smile tugged at his lips. "Um, toast? Although, I think tonight, we'll refer to it as garlic bread." That earned him a laugh from the other two conspirators in my life.

I gave in. "Fine, fine. Can I at least make a salad? Will you all trust me to do that much?"

Cal nodded. "No objection from me. I'm not going to eat salad anyway."

"Me either."

I stuck my tongue out at the two men. "Traitors. Both of you." I pointed to Moose as well. "Don't you think I missed that smirk on your face either, Hound. I'll be rationing your treats a little more from now on." Moose's response was to drop his head to the floor and cover his eyes with his two front paws, inciting more laughter.

I didn't say anything else, my back to them as I threw a quick salad together for myself. Tonight, things were good between the four of us, and it felt right.

Chapter Four

WHEN I WOKE the next morning, my house was oddly quiet. Moose still slept at the foot of my bed. He liked to sneak up there after I fell asleep each night. I pretended to be surprised every time I found him curled up by my feet, the warmth and weight of him an extra comfort on the nights my sleep wasn't so restful.

Normally, he'd stretch as soon as I did, yawning wide enough that I could count all his teeth if I wanted to. But today, things were different. Something felt off. A quick glance at the clock let me know I was awake almost a full hour before my alarm was set to go off. I shuffled to the door of my room and paused, listening to the minute sounds of my house as it settled incrementally. Most days, Cal would be awake before me and already downstairs, brewing his precious coffee and making a breakfast he would cajole me into eating. Instead, it was quiet downstairs.

I shoved my hair out of my eyes and reached for a sweatshirt to combat the chill. Winter in Nebraska meant that I had to do whatever I could to ward off the cold. It was one of the side effects of choosing not to carry a piece of Hell inside me. I'd learned to live with it. I slipped on socks and shoes, then headed down the stairs to the living room. Nothing appeared to have been disturbed. I made my way into the kitchen, pulling out tea to brew myself a cup. As I waited, I watched out the windows, looking for any sign of movement. Anything that might explain the uneasy feeling creeping up the back of my neck.

When the water was hot and the tea had steeped long enough that I could smell its strong, heady scent, I picked the mug up off the counter and took a trial sip. Cal loved his coffee, but for me, nothing was as good as this. I closed my eyes, enjoying the chance to indulge in my morning ritual alone for the first time in months. A few more sips and I felt ready to face whatever the day might throw at me.

I finished my tea and rinsed the mug out, setting it in the sink. I turned to go back upstairs when something outside caught my eye. Or, something missing. I reached the window and looked to where Torren's car had been parked every day since he'd joined us. It was gone, the ruts from his tires clearly visible. I ran to the living room, shoving the blinds out of the way in my haste.

"Maybe they moved it and you weren't paying attention,"

I whispered the words to myself as I looked for his car through the front windows. But it wasn't there.

Torren was gone.

※

CAL FACED ME ACROSS the kitchen table while Moose stretched out over the top of my feet. For some reason, having him there was comforting, and I was pretty sure he knew that.

"Did he say anything to you before? Mention leaving at all?"

I nodded, my hands shaking as I held the note we'd found in Torren's room. "Yesterday he offered to leave with me. Said we could go anywhere I wanted to. I told him that wouldn't work. That you and Angus would be able to find us." I looked down at the bracelet that covered the scars on my left wrist. It was beautifully intricate, roses tooled into the leather, red gems catching the light. Angus had gifted the four of us with these, crafted specifically for the individual. The one Moose wore as his collar was able to shift with him as he changed forms. Tor had left his behind, tossed onto the bed.

"Did you want to go?" He asked the question softly, surprising me.

"I, well, no. I didn't want to leave. This is my home. Why would I want to leave it?" I met his gaze, my jaw stubbornly set. I'd lost the home I'd grown up in when the powers I'd inherited became a threat to those around me. I had no intention of giving this one up. Not willingly.

He looked down at the tabletop, running his hands over the grain. "I know I haven't been the easiest to work with lately. And, I've been pushing you really hard. I want to make sure you're ready. For whatever's coming."

I reached across the table, grabbing his hand, suddenly afraid he would leave too. "You've done everything you could, everything that's been asked of you. I'm a better fighter now. I've got more control of my magic. And we're all learning to manage the rest of it. At least it seemed like we were."

He squeezed my fingers in return. "Then we'll keep working. For now, let's give Torren a few days. There's no sign he was taken against his will. The wards were still active when we checked them this morning. He probably needs some space, to think about things. Our world can be hard for humans to adjust to. Going after him could make things worse."

I sighed. "You're probably right. But what if something happens to him because of us?"

"Delaney, I know you don't want to hear this, but it's the truth. You won't be able to protect him from everything. Even if he was here with us, he could still get hurt. It's the nature of things."

"True." I'd seen that exact thing happen not that long ago. We'd been fighting a Golem that had attacked while

Torren and Callum were walking the property, checking for any weaknesses. I'd found a way to blow it apart, but the explosion had thrown Tor several feet through the air, his head hitting one of the ward stones that guarded the house when he landed. Even then, my attempt to protect us all had been the very thing that injured him.

"Let's stick to our routine for now. Give him time to figure things out. If he isn't back in a week, we'll check on him. Fair enough?"

Cal's suggestion was completely reasonable. "Okay, we'll handle it your way. For now."

"Good. Now, go get changed. Might as well get our workout done for today. You've got training to do."

I growled at him as I passed by. "Slave driver."

His laughter followed me out of the kitchen.

Chapter Five

THE VISIT WE'D been expecting came two days later. Uncle Newt appeared in my backyard as we were finishing our dinner. Cal and Moose went out to greet him, while I waited inside, chewing at the edge of a rough fingernail. I was anxious, wondering what Newt needed from us. What we'd be asked to do. We still hadn't heard anything from Torren, and I couldn't seem to stop myself from worrying. I'd habitually check our currently unbreakable bond, the connection we'd accidentally forged months ago. If I closed my eyes, I could see it more clearly. The color of it was still bright, none of the darkness I'd come to associate with an unhealthy bond. But I wasn't feeling anything from it. The flares of emotion I'd gotten from him right before he'd left were gone. Maybe the distance was helping him. I hoped that was true.

The sound of the door opening brought my eyes open. I

was self-conscious about being caught testing the bond. The look on Cal's face when he walked in told me he'd already guessed what I'd been doing. He hadn't discouraged me from it, but he'd done his best to keep me busy and distracted since Tor's disappearance. He worried about me.

"Hey there, Uncle Newt." I greeted my father's best friend with a quick kiss to his stubbled cheek and a hug. "What's got you visiting us today?"

Cal and Newt exchanged a look. Moose trotted over to his bed and curled up in it, his watchful gaze on all of us. Finally, it was Cal who broke the news.

"Newt found out the location of a small group of rogue demons. They've refused to answer the call to return Below. There have been humans involved. Your father would like us to go take care of them."

This is what Angus had wanted me to be trained for. Not only to be able to defend myself, but to seek out the demons who were rebelling and exact his punishment. There was a dose of irony in his plan that hadn't escaped me. Still, I wasn't going to sit by and let demons prey on humans. There was only one question. "Are we planning to do this without Torren?"

Cal nodded. "No sense waiting for him to come back. I think the three of us can handle this. You've come a long way in your training. And every day we wait means more people could be hurt."

"Fine. When do we need to leave?"

Newt passed an address to me. I glanced at it and handed it to Callum. "Tonight," Newt said. "They're supposed to be at that address for the next couple days, but Angus doesn't want to wait." He paused, looking at his feet before focusing back on me. "He wants them to be an example to other demons. Don't hold back."

With that, he said his goodbyes and then made his way out the back door. I watched as he disappeared, heading back Below to confer with my father, no doubt.

"You feel okay with this happening tonight?" asked Cal, bringing me back to reality. I hadn't realized I was staring out the window at the spot where Newt had been until I heard Cal's voice.

"Yes," I said, my voice firm. "This is what Angus has had you training me for, so I'd be ready if he needed help. At least he's not keeping me in the dark all the time, to keep me safe."

"Do you feel ready?"

I was surprised by the question. "You see me every day. If you're worried that I can't handle this, you should've mentioned that before Uncle Newt left."

"Don't get defensive, Laney." He held his hands up, his sign he wanted a truce for the moment. "You're upset about Torren being gone; I know that. And, I'm not doubting your ability. I'm asking if you feel you're ready for this. Angus is asking a lot of you. I want to make sure you're going to be okay with what happens."

I gave his words some thought. Before we'd met, I'd hunted down a Chaos Demon that had been murdering women. I'd not only put the plan in place, but I'd stopped him. He wouldn't be hurting any more women. But that's not what Callum was thinking about. His concern was that, for the first time, my father was giving me instructions to hunt down demons and kill them. For him. He was turning me into an assassin.

"I'm not going to lie and tell you I enjoy killing. But I also won't sit by and do nothing while humans are being hurt. I can't. Not when I can stop that from happening."

Cal nodded, his eyes searching mine. Then he gave me a small smile, the crooked one I thought was adorable and a little sad at the same time. "All right then. Go get ready. Remember, sensible shoes."

I laughed as I left him behind, throwing a sarcastic reminder back at him over my shoulder. "Hey now, I've only fought a demon in heels once. And I won."

Chapter Six

Cal's portal took us to an alley behind a restaurant about two blocks away from the address Newt had given us. He'd used a picture of the restaurant we found online to link the portal to the location. Closing time had come and gone, so there wasn't anyone around to see us. Calling a portal without an idea of where you needed to go was apparently a very bad idea. At least, that's how he explained it to me.

We walked the rest of the way, me in my very sensible shoes. Moose walked beside us. Before we left the house, he'd shifted into the form of an oversized Yorkie. His sleek black fur turned a caramel brown with a stripe of silver down his back even as he began to shrink. When he was done, the pony-sized Hell Hound had become a sweet terrier, from the tips of his perked-up ears to the end of his stubbed little tail. The transformation was as fascinating for me to watch as it had been the very first time.

When we arrived at the address we'd been given, I was surprised to see the house was completely dark. We'd expected there to be signs someone was here, but as we circled the dwelling, there was no indication anyone was inside. There was a sense of abandonment hanging around the building, as if it'd been empty for a long time.

We found a good vantage point and settled down onto the ground to watch and wait. Moose pressed himself close, the warmth of him radiating into me. I rested my hand on the silky fur at the top of his head. Having Callum and Moose with me for this assignment was vastly different than the first time I'd gone demon hunting. I knew we'd all watch out for each other, no matter what happened. Before, I'd been alone. Looking between them, I decided that having a team to work with was much better than being on my own.

After an hour of no movement or sound, we decided to find a way in and see what we could find inside. Maybe the demons we were looking for had already come and gone, leaving some evidence behind that could point us to where they could be found.

Moose went first, sneaking through the unkept yard. He stayed in the shadows, naturally flowing with them as they shifted. I lost sight of him as he reached the foundation of the home, blending into the darkness there. Cal urged me on, and I followed the same path I'd seen Moose take, using the darkness as cover. When I made it to the side of the house, I leaned against it and tried to calm the racing of my heart. There was a chuffing sound behind me, and I froze. When the wet nose nudged my ear, I relaxed and choked down the laugh that threatened to escape. Moose had shifted back into his Hell Hound form. He licked my cheek and I gave him a playful shove on the shoulder. We needed to be serious.

Once Callum joined us, we made our way to the back door of the dwelling. It was completely shadowed, no streetlights nearby and no nosy neighbors with their porches lit up. The door wasn't locked, and it opened easily, the only noise the clicking of the latch as we shut it carefully behind us.

We entered a short hallway, dark as night. Not wanting to turn on any lights, we let Moose lead the way, trusting his canine eyesight. He slipped ahead, his head turning at every tiny sound, ears cocked as he listened. When he looked back at us and bobbed his head, we knew it was safe to keep going.

We cleared the entire main floor, leaving only the second floor and the basement to be investigated. Pausing, I leaned in close to Cal and whispered, "I'll check the basement."

He drew back, then nodded and pointed to Moose, who gave a sigh. I assumed that meant he'd been assigned to accompany me downstairs. As Callum headed up the stairs to the second floor, Moose and I paused at the open doorway that led down. The darkness beneath us was oppressive. I let Moose proceed down the stairs first, following close behind. The stairs creaked with each step I took, the sound loud in my ears, compared to how silent Moose was.

I joined my Hound at the landing. He pressed himself tight to my side and I laced my fingers through his collar. The simple contact gave me comfort and renewed confidence. As if in response, the depth of the darkness pressed in on us, a heavy weight to the air. The chill I'd expected being underground was missing. Instead, there was an unnatural warmth and an odor rose up, the mingled scents of fear and rot, strong enough that I gagged.

Moose stepped forward and I followed beside him, unwilling to lose contact with him. The floor was hard-packed earth, likely the original cellar from when the dwelling was first built. I held my hand out and whispered, a flicker of flame appearing on my palm. I pursed my lips and whistled softly, my breath lifting the flame and carrying it into the air, where it swayed on the current, lighting our way. As we moved forward, so did the flame, throwing a soft glow ahead. This was a practical trick I'd worked on. Moose might be able to see in the dark, but I was essentially blind without at least some sort of illumination.

We searched the first room, checking all the corners carefully and finding nothing. It all felt wrong. There was something off about the basement but I couldn't nail down what it was. An unnatural heat filled the space. Despite the warmth, my skin was clammy, and a chill was creeping up my neck. The bundle of flame floating in the air before us dipped suddenly, as if caught in a draft.

Moose growled, the sound vibrating up my arm. I pulled

in a shaky breath. The odor we'd noticed when we first stepped into the basement swelled and bile filled the back of my throat. I forced myself to swallow it back down. I refused to throw up down here.

In the light from the flames, I saw the outline of a door to our left. Together, Moose and I made our way to it. Heat radiated out around the wood frame and I lifted my hand to turn the knob.

The door bowed in as if sensing my presence. I froze. Shock coursed through me as cracks appeared in the wood frame. The pressure dropped and the flames I'd created went out, air rushing by us. The hinges squealed as they succumbed to the force of the vacuum on the other side of the doorway. Then it was gone, the space where it had been gaping open, revealing a large room lit only by a jagged blood red slash in the air. It was as if something had torn a hole in space, allowing Hell access to the world above. Shadows moved in the center of that rift, and a growl rolled out from it. I took a step back without thinking, some instinctual part of me recognizing I shouldn't go into that room. More movement caught my eye and I saw the room was filled with demons. Who all turned and looked at me.

Chapter Seven

I IMMEDIATELY shifted, blocking the demons' view of my Hound. He whined and nudged my hip, but I didn't move. He'd protected me many times before. I needed to keep him safe from the snarling faces that had focused on us.

"Back up," I whispered, waving my hand at him. I wanted to give us room to work and make sure we had access to an escape route. I also didn't want any demons sneaking up on us from behind.

Moose did as I asked and I followed, sliding my feet carefully so I wouldn't trip or stumble. The glaring red eyes of the demons followed our movements. We had crossed half the distance to the stairs when a whipcord-thin figure appeared in the middle of the crimson light, cloaked in black, arms raised. The figure shrieked, the sound distorting in the air. The horde instantly began to advance toward us as if that was their signal to attack. The door frame was still in place, cracked and bent. I hoped it would act as a natural barrier that would funnel them into a tight group if they continued. I was counting on it.

Moose let loose a deep, rolling bark that vibrated the air. Dirt fell from the rafters above us in response and I prayed that Cal had felt it all the way up on the second floor. An alarm to let him know we'd need his help.

The demons continued to the doorway. I frantically tried to catalog what types of demons we were facing, but there were so many. I caught sight of the long, slender bodies of Sirens beside the bone-gray skin of Proles Demons, hunters of children. The hard, handsome planes of the faces of Chaos Demons were recognizable next to the stunning beauty of Incubi. And many more. All had the telltale hint of red in their hair and a murderous glint in their hard eyes.

I tried to look past them, for the humans reported to have been at risk, but there were none I could see. As the first group reached the doorway, I relaxed, knowing they would have to form up into a column to come at us. This would allow me to strike fast and focused, right down the middle.

Except it didn't work that way. As the first demon breached the threshold, the frame of the door warped and expanded, stretching wide and allowing the front row to step through together.

"Well, Hells," I muttered under my breath. "Didn't expect that at all."

Moose nudged me again, tipping his head toward the stairs when I looked down at him. I got the message. He wanted us to make a break for it, back to the first floor.

I nodded at him. "Okay, you first." He growled, narrowing his black eyes me, but I refused to give in. "No. You go first. I'll be right behind you."

Huffing in disgust, Moose turned and dashed to the stairs, the sound of his nails skittering across the wood telling me he'd made it. I looked back to the group of demons, fear pooling in my belly at the distance they'd already crossed and how many of them there were. I needed a way to slow them down.

Closing my eyes, I pulled up the power I carried within me. When it had gathered in response, I gave it direction and purpose. A shield appeared, a nearly invisible barrier that spread across the room, forcing the demons to stop their advance toward me.

I smiled, a word of thanks to the magic whispered in my mind. I took a moment to examine the demons again as they came up against my shield, seeking a way through or around. Some hammered on it. Others tested it with their brands of magic. The bloody slash still hung in the air in the room they'd come from, but the cloaked figure was gone. And I still hadn't seen any humans, endangered or otherwise. It made me wonder what this gathering had been for.

Moose gave a harsh bark, the fear I could hear in the sound grabbing my attention. I spun around. A new rift had appeared directly behind me, arms reaching to grasp at my clothes. I stumbled back, wrenching myself away. My focus wavered. I heard a shriek from the demons, confirmation that my shield must have suffered from my distraction. I twisted around on my knees, crawling toward the shield, doubling the energy I'd originally poured into it. I could see cracks spreading through the field of power that held the demons back, places where claws had broken through. I shot a glance over my shoulder. The rift swelled, growing wider and giving whoever waited on the other side more reach and range of motion. And it was between me and my chance at escape up the stairs.

Moose howled, coiling himself to jump over the railing to me. I shook my head, screaming at him to stay there, but he ignored me. He leapt, soaring through the air and landing beside me. I pushed up to a standing position, my hand on his back, his stance firm and focused. My protector. And I was his.

I focused on my power once again, desperation fueling me. The demons were breaking through my original shield. With Moose right next to me, we didn't need a wide area of protection. It only had to be strong and focused. I let the original shield drop, ignoring the victorious cries as it fell. Instead, I scribed a circle in the air, and directed the power to form a new shield. One that completely surrounded me and my Hound.

It popped into place as the first demons made it to us.

They hit it hard and the percussive impact rattled through me. Confident it would hold them, I examined the new rift which had widened enough that I could see the cloaked figure that had been in the other room. It had reached through to snare me before, but now it was still, waiting as it watched the scene, a detached air about it. I couldn't see a face, not even a hint of eyes, but the feeling that its attention was focused solely on me wouldn't go away. My hands curled into fists as I faced it down, refusing to give in or look away. I stayed that way until my view of the cloaked figure was blocked by the bodies of demons surging around our shelter. They piled up, cutting through each other as they fought to break through the shield. The red light around us dimmed as the demons crowded in and I hunched down onto the floor, one hand buried in Moose's fur. His unwavering presence calmed me, and an idea began to push forward to the front of mind.

I gave Moose a quick hug, breathing in the comforting scent of him, a mix of spicy brimstone and canine. I looked him in the eye and promised him one thing. "We're going to get through this. Stay close to me."

Moose licked my nose in response, then faced the demons around us and curled his upper lip, a snarl pouring from him. The demons screamed in response, doubling their efforts to take down the shield I held around us.

Cal's training had forced me to always be thinking during a battle. I'd followed his favorite mantra, understanding why he believed that defense is the very best offense. We were safe within the bubble of security I'd built. For now. But I wouldn't be able to hold it forever. And I didn't know when Cal might come looking for us. I had to prepare for my next critical move. The one I believed would save us.

I closed my eyes once again, envisioning the shield I held in place around us. Keeping that visual firm in my mind, I pulled up my power again, letting it build layer by layer as it spilled out of a well deep within me. The screams of the demons were louder. I felt the shield shudder under their repeated blows. Still, I waited. I needed every demon as close as possible before I struck out at them.

The power continued to build in answer to my call. I felt stretched from within, my skin burning with the strain of holding the energy tight inside. The shield shook around us. Large cracks spiderwebbed across it, the apparent success of their onslaught whipping the demons up into a frenzy. A claw cut through, swiping across my ankle. Moose growled, lunging forward but I pulled him back with my hand tight in his fur. He had to stay next to me.

A hot river of pain flared along the back of my leg, a second demon sneaking a hand through and reaching for me. I held tight, forcing the magic to wait a little longer, promising it would be free soon. Another claw sunk in and I fought against the agony, my body trembling with power.

I felt it when the shield finally gave. The energy I'd siphoned into it bounced back and joined with the magic I'd gathered into my core. Moose yelped, his body going rigid under my hand as a scream escaped me. I dropped to my knees, wrapped my arms around him and held on tight. Magic burst free when I released it, bowing my back, and I felt something snap. Bright light flared, followed by a rolling wave as the explosion roared around us. I kept my grip on Moose, his strength the only thing holding me up as the energy raced away, destroying everything in its path.

The structure above us groaned and dust rained down. I took a deep breath to steady myself, but my muscles gave out, shaking from the exertion. I dimly heard my name being called but didn't have the energy to lift my head. Moose's warm breath drifted over my face and joy filled me knowing I'd saved him. The floor beneath me tipped and my grip faltered, sliding across sleek fur. Hands caught me before I hit the hard ground, and Cal's face swam into view, worry written across his features. Even in the darkness, he seemed to glow, and I smiled, something wet spilling out of my mouth with the motion.

"Laney, we're getting out of here." He pulled me close, my face in his chest. I drank in the feeling of his arms around me. He hadn't held me in a very long time. Sadness pulsed, awareness of how much I'd missed this connection with him settling over me.

The pressure in the air changed, telling me that a portal had opened. I struggled to get my legs under me, to stand on my own, but they wouldn't respond to my command.

Cal's arms tightened around me as he whispered in my ear. "Shh, I've got you." He gathered me up, one arm under my knees as the other supported my shoulders. Holding me tight against his chest, I heard the deep rumble of his voice as he ordered Moose to enter the portal first.

Then it was our turn, the wind around us spiraling faster as we neared the entrance. "Laney, I need you to hold on until we get home. Hold on a little bit longer." My body was tired, and my heart stuttered in my chest, dropping a beat. I wanted to rest, to let go of everything. My hands fell from around his neck, going limp. His grip tightened, fingers digging in. "Hang on, damn it. You will hang on." This time, he'd layered magic into his words, a command, and even though I wanted to give in, to let the promise of rest take me, I couldn't resist doing as he asked.

Chapter Eight

I WOKE IN MY BED, warm arms around me. The press of a hard chest against my bare back was surprising and, at the same time, comforting. A mound of blankets was piled on top of me and I could distantly hear Moose snoring. I was safe and, by all indications, healed.

When I shifted, the arms around me tightened, pulling me flush to the front of him. I didn't try to pull away. I knew who held me, who had healed me. Callum.

His words were low in my ear as he whispered. "Hells, Laney, please don't ever do something like that again." There was an undercurrent in his voice, fear and need, that filled me with sadness.

"I'll do my best," I said, trying to keep my response light. "I hadn't exactly planned on needing to do it in the first place."

He dropped his lips to my shoulder, pressing a gentle

kiss there. "I'm not joking, Laney. I wasn't sure I could bring you back this time."

My heart sped up at the sound of his voice, at the simple kiss he'd given me. We'd been circling each other for what had felt like forever, unsure how to move forward after I'd betrayed his trust. To finally be here, in his arms again, was wonderful. I didn't want to ruin this moment, to break this contact with him. So, I didn't. I relaxed into his embrace. He trailed his fingers down my arm, a silky touch that kindled a new heat in my core.

"I'm sorry." I almost missed the words, he said them so softly, his lips moving across my skin.

I tried not to flinch, but it was hard to keep myself still. "What are you apologizing for? You saved my life."

There was a hitch in his breathing before he answered, and I ached to turn and face him. "For pushing you away. I've been hard on you, holding you at a distance. I didn't realize how much you leaving me behind before hurt."

I twisted around, unable to wait any longer. His eyes were beautifully sad as they met mine. The need to push his hurt away surged within my chest and I laid my hands on his stubbled cheeks, framing his mouth on both sides. "I'm sorry, too," I said. "Now we're even." I pulled his lips to mine in a kiss I'd been dreaming about for far too long.

He froze for a moment and I hesitated, afraid I'd overstepped a boundary he didn't want breached, but then he was kissing me in return. There was a freedom in being able to do this with him. He'd shown me once before that I didn't have to be guarded with him, that my magic didn't have the same effect on him as it did on other people. He was the one man in the world I could kiss and not have to worry that I'd ruin his life by binding us together forever.

I twined my hands into his hair as he shifted, his teeth nipping playfully at my lips. I wanted to tease him, the words already forming in my head, but then his tongue skated along the seam of my mouth and whatever I'd planned to say escaped me. I opened for him and my heart sped as his kiss turned from a simple exploration into a deep, complete connection.

When he finally broke away, my pulse was pounding in my ears and I couldn't catch my breath. I reached for him, wanting to pull him back down even though I was abruptly aware of the lack of clothing between us. He grabbed my hand, dropping a kiss to my knuckles, before looking back over his shoulder toward the door of my bedroom.

"Hang on. Did you hear something?"

I shook my head, unable to hear anything but my heart.

Cal waited, holding himself still above me. I took advantage and drank in the sight of him. Muscles forged from hours of hard training, skin that gleamed golden. He was a work of art. When my gaze found its way back to his face, he was grinning, as if he was appreciating my appraisal, confident he would be found acceptable.

"Like what you see?" he asked, his voice husky.

I laughed. "You'll do," I said, reaching up for him, wanting his lips on mine once again.

He let me pull him down, sealed his lips to mine and then we were interrupted. By a knock at the front door.

Chapter Nine

CAL PULLED AWAY from me again, this time with a muttered curse. A pleased flush spread over me at the disappointment I could feel spilling from him. It was a powerful feeling, to know I had this effect on him. I untangled myself from the sheets and left the warmth of my bed behind.

"Um, you might want to put some clothes on before you go down there." Cal's voice brushed over me, teasing and happy, and my heart resumed its galloping pace.

I turned to him, my hands on my hips. He sat on the bed, one knee under him, leaning back on one hand, his eyes roving over me. I pointed at him. "You might want to take your own advice. Nobody's going to believe we were like this just so you could heal me."

His lips twitched at that. "I never said it was just so I could heal you."

I threw the shirt I'd pulled out of a drawer at him.

"Well, that's our story and we're sticking to it. Now, go get some clothes on you so I can focus."

He tossed the shirt back to me and climbed off my bed. Another knock sounded from downstairs and I forced my mind away from Cal to focus on more immediate concerns. Like who was at my door. I didn't have unexpected visitors all that often, and on the rare occasions they did show up, it usually meant something was wrong.

I tugged the shirt on, grabbed a pair of sweatpants and yanked them up around my waist. I didn't bother to run a brush through my hair. Whoever waited outside would have to take me as I was.

I pulled the door of my bedroom open to find Moose laying in the hallway. He lifted his head from the floor to look at me, curiosity in the way he quirked his head, as if he was asking why I was getting out of bed.

"Not much of a guard dog today, are you?" I teased him. "Someone's at the door and you're laying here like there's nothing to worry about." I reached down and gave him a playful smack on the rump. "Come on, lazy dog. Let's go see who that is."

He clambered to his feet and followed me down the stairs. By the time we'd reached the living room, he'd shifted from his full-size Hell Hound form into his smaller Yorkie appearance. He looked much less threatening like that. I put my hand on the door, checking to make sure he was ready for any threat. He huffed and lifted a lip, showing me the teeth he sported in this form. They would still do some damage in a confrontation. I grinned at him. "Tough guy, aren't you? Okay then, here we go."

I clicked over the dead bolt, the sound of it releasing loud in the quiet of the house. I pulled open the door, holding my hand up to block the glare of the early morning sun. A figure stepped into view and I froze as recognition settled over me. Torren Bishop was standing on my front porch. He was back.

⚡

Torren looked down at me, eyes tired and hair thrown about by the Nebraska wind.

"Hey, Laney. Mind if I come in?"

The bond between us pulsed, the connection strong again now that he was close, and I could feel the conflicting emotions running through him. Hope that I would let him in, fear that I would turn him away.

For a moment, I couldn't move. My own feelings were at war with each other. He'd left us, without a word about why or if he'd be back. A part of me wanted to slam the door in his face but a larger piece of me was glad he'd come home.

A sound on the stairs made me turn, the door swinging wide with my movement. Cal stopped where he was as he saw Torren standing outside. His eyes met mine and I watched as the relaxed, comfortable Callum I'd been kissing a few moments earlier was replaced by the one who was all business. The muscles in his jaw tensed and he gripped the stair railing so hard, I thought I heard it creak in protest.

We hung there, the three of us suspended in the taut tension that pulsed through the air, not sure what our next move should be. It was Moose who broke us free, coming to me and leaning his small form against my leg. He gave a soft huff and then went to Torren, sitting down at his feet.

Tor reached down, petting the Hound between the ears. "It's good to see you, too, Moose." A small smile on his lips, he looked back up to me. "So, what do you think? Can I come in?"

I shot a glance to Cal, but his face betrayed nothing. He was leaving this decision for me to make. I wanted to reach out to him, his strength bolstering mine as I chose how the four of us would move forward. But it didn't really matter. There was only one choice I could make.

I swung the door wide open with a sigh. "Yeah. You can."

Torren gave a relieved smile and some of the strain eased from his shoulders as he stepped over the threshold. I felt an answering relief in my center as the bond between us registered the most important fact. Tor had come home.

Chapter Ten

I WAS SEATED at the kitchen table, a hot mug of tea steeping in my hands. Cal fussed with his fancy coffee beans, imported from Indonesia or some other place where the volcanic soil provided the perfect growing matrix. He'd told me once, but I couldn't remember all the details. He insisted on hand-grinding the beans, which he would then add to his French press with filtered water boiled in an electric tea kettle. Those contraptions took up a sizable amount of my counter space, but I didn't mind. It was a ritual for him. For all of us really. The scent of his coffee in the air every morning was reassuring to me after these last few months, a reminder that all was as it should be. But, I could tell he was using it to draw out the inevitable confrontation that waited. Moose crunched on his breakfast, while Torren stood in the corner, his eyes on the three of us. It was surprising how our rhythm had adjusted so quickly while he was gone. I knew we'd get back to the way things used to be, but for the time being, it was uncomfortable.

Callum was the first to break the silence. He turned to face Torren, leaning back against the counter and crossing his arms over his chest. "So, you mind telling us why you left? Or better yet, why you're back?"

It was a challenge, simple and direct. I wanted the answers to those questions myself, so I didn't object or interfere. Torren had some things he needed to explain to earn his way back into our good graces.

Tor shuffled his feet, the toe of his boot nudging the gray backpack he'd dropped to the floor when he'd come in. "There were some things I needed to take care of. They couldn't wait any longer."

I thought of the telephone conversation I'd had with a woman he worked with, when I was first trying to get a sense of who Torren Bishop actually was. She'd asked if I was one of his girls, women he'd helped escape dangerous situations. Was that why he'd left? To help them?

Cal and I didn't say anything. He stood firm, his eyes hard as we waited for Torren to continue. The only sound interrupting the silence was Moose as he devoured his food.

Tor finally gave in. "Look, I needed to wrap up some things. There were people depending on me. I've got them sorted now, but I couldn't take care of them from here. Had to be done in person."

I nodded, my eyes on my tea, my finger tracing the rim

of the mug. What he said next brought my head up in surprise.

"And... I needed to resign my position with the police department. Another thing I felt should be done in person." There was a distinct pain underlying those words. A pain that matched the look on his face.

"You didn't have to do that," I said, wishing I could reach out to him, offer him some comfort. I understood what this sacrifice meant to him, how it felt to leave everything that mattered to you behind. But I held back. Hurt I hadn't realized was there blazed to life inside my chest and I rubbed the spot, as if I could physically ease the ache pulsing behind my breastbone.

His eyes met mine as he gave me a sad smile. "Yes, I did."

The bond between us opened and I felt the twinge of regret and loss spiraling from him into me. Out of instinct, I shielded myself from the impact of his emotions. Torren flinched, his shoulders slumping as I cut our connection. I hadn't needed to be on guard while he was gone. This was going to take some getting used to again.

I picked up my mug and stood up from the table. Moose paused his eating to watch as I crossed the room. Before I left the kitchen, I looked back at Torren. "Welcome home," I said, then left him with Callum and Moose. I needed some time alone to adjust to what it felt like with Tor so close again.

Torren tried to call me back. "Laney, wait, I'm sorry. I

should've told you what I was doing. I know that now. Please, let's talk about this."

I didn't turn around, my breathing ragged as I tried to find my center again. It was Cal's voice that followed me this time, but he wasn't calling me back. Instead, he offered Torren a warning. "If you do this to her ever again, I swear on all the Hells, I *will* kill you."

⚡

I WENT FOR A WALK outside, needing the distance and separation. Torren had only just returned, and the house was already feeling claustrophobic with the four of us in it. I didn't venture far, but I needed some time away and checking the ward stones was the perfect excuse. They vibrated strongly, the magic that powered them almost tangible as I rested my hand on the top of one of them. The magic spread up into me, warm and familiar. These stones had been my guardians since I'd moved here. They were a constant.

The flavor of the magic had changed slightly though, mine but amplified. Cal's doing, I assumed. The man could work wonders with magic. I needed to ask him how he did that. There were still things I needed to know, but we never seemed to have a chance to talk about them.

I turned my attention to the acres that spread out around my home. It was a peaceful place, even now, with winter firmly entrenched. There were years of history here, family roots established long before I arrived. This place had lived many lives. My own was simply another one passing through. It would continue on without me if need be.

Chapter Eleven

CALLUM MET ME at the back door, holding it open so I could step right into the kitchen. I stripped off my winter coat and draped it over the back of a chair. There was no sign of Torren.

"Here, drink this. It'll warm you up." Cal handed me a fresh cup of tea, steam rising from it. I took a sip and savored the taste, the way it soothed me instantly. The house was quiet.

Cal answered the question I didn't ask. "Tor's upstairs. Passed out in his bed before he even got his shoes off. He'll sleep for a while, I'd guess. Worn out by everything."

"Because of me?" My words were hesitant, the fear of what he might say weighing them down.

He sighed. "No Laney, not because of you. Because of the bond. The farther away he was, the more it drained him. At least, I'm assuming that's what was going on. Your energy never seemed affected while he was gone, but he's not like you. He doesn't know how to manage it, can't control it the way you do, so it was harder for him."

"Did it hurt him?" My voice broke and I wiped away a tear that was threatening to spill from my eye.

Callum's arm settled around me, tugging me into his side. "Not that I could tell. Just tired, is all. He'll be all right."

I rested my head against him, comforted by the feeling of him holding me there. Already, things between us were different, shifting from our intimately close morning encounter to a distance we had to maintain. It was too hard on Torren otherwise. Cal and I had been born to magic, to a world where it had always existed. Tor had been dragged into this, his whole life disrupted by circumstances outside his control.

Cal dropped a kiss on my forehead. "Might as well get ready for training," he said, his arm easing away from me, as if he was reluctant to let me go. He straightened to his full height, his posture shifting as he physically returned to his role as my instructor. "I've got a feeling we're going to need it. And no doubt we'll have to report to Angus about what happened."

"Are you going to tell him what I did?"

"I don't think I'll need to tell him much. You left a crater in that basement. The house was about to cave in when we left. I'm pretty sure he'll know that already." Cal's voice shifted, going from teasing to heavily serious. "But I'll try to leave out the part about you almost dying. He gets upset when he hears about that sort of thing."

We spent the rest of the morning battling it out in the training room. Cal took it easier on me, which I appreciated after the previous night's events. Considering what I'd done, I was surprised by how good I felt. Moving helped me work through the pain and stiffness that still lingered. Moose watched from the sidelines, a doggy kind of grin on his face as we focused on hand-to-hand fighting. Magic was a handy thing to have, but so was a good upper cut. When you were able to use physical strength in tandem with a boost of magic, your offensive options expanded. Cal forced me to think on my feet every time we fought, to adjust to his quickly changing tactics. To use magic in different ways to amplify my fighting skills.

Sparring was one of my favorite things to do and I lost myself in the rhythm of the fight. Cal was a tough opponent, so every time I broke through his guard and made contact with him, I considered it an accomplishment. He also challenged me to work on my own defensive moves, throwing in tricks when I could.

As he came forward, I slid to the left and hooked his ankle. He lost his balance and my fist connected with the pads on his chest, sending him falling backward onto the mat. He shook his head, as if he needed to clear it, and then grinned up at me. "Well done, Laney. I didn't see that one coming."

I blushed, appreciating the high praise. "I had a good teacher. He knocked me on my butt a couple times with that move."

He climbed back to his feet, rubbing the spot where I'd hit him. "I felt that punch all the way through the pads. You've definitely gotten stronger."

"Good to know all this work is finally paying off," I said. Sweat trickled down my forehead and I swiped it away. "Are we done? Or do we need to keep going?"

Cal smiled. "Go ahead and get cleaned up. I think you've earned a break." He glanced over at Moose, who'd jumped to attention as if he'd heard something above us. "And it looks like we've got company. Time to check in."

Chapter Twelve

I WAS EXPECTING to see Angus, but it was Uncle Newt who waited for us in the kitchen. He nibbled on a cookie that looked suspiciously like the ones Cal liked to snack on.

"These are good," he said, holding it up for inspection. "Might have to take a few with me for the road. There's never enough cookies Below, in my opinion."

"Hey, Uncle Newt," I gave him a quick hug, aware of the sweat dripping from me. "It's good to see you again."

He surveyed me as I stepped back. "You don't look any worse for wear. I'm assuming that means everything went well last night."

Cal answered the unspoken question. "If by well you mean there were at least triple the number of demons we were expecting, and that Delaney destroyed them all, then sure. Everything went perfectly fine."

I looked at him, surprised he'd known how many

demons there were. He shrugged at me. "Moose is a very good witness. And despite popular belief, Hell Hounds do know how to count."

Newt laughed at that comment, dropping his eyes to look at my Hound. "Well done, Moose. I knew Angus sending you to Laney was a good idea. I trust you're still happy here?"

Moose tipped his head forward once, a move I assumed was an affirmation. Then he laid down at Cal's feet. They were an aligned front, these companions of mine.

"Good to know." Newt turned his attention back to me and Cal. "Now, any evidence left behind, or did you get away clean?"

I couldn't answer that question, not really being conscious when we left the place. Thankfully, Cal stepped in again. "If you consider clean to be a smoking crater in the basement and a house about to collapse then yeah, it was as clean as could be." Cal's voice was coated with tightly leashed fury.

Newt narrowed his eyes at Cal. "You sound like there's something else you want to say. Might as well get it out there, Callum."

"That was a crap job you sent us on, Newt, and you know it. Bad intel to start with. More targets than we could be expected to handle on our own. Something's happening and we're not being told everything. It's too risky."

Newt pointed to me. "And yet, Laney seems to have

come through it fine. So much so, she was working out with you like it was any other day."

"She almost died!" Cal's voice broke, his hands fisted at his sides. His eyes were furious, and I was afraid for a moment that he was going to lunge at Uncle Newt, maybe even hit him. "If I hadn't been there, if I hadn't gotten to her when I did, she wouldn't have survived. It took everything I had to heal her this time. Make sure you tell Angus that, Newton. See what he thinks of this idea when he knows what could've happened."

Newt leaned forward in his chair, his elbows on his knees. "Why do you think you're here, Callum? To serve a purpose. Nothing more. Do not forget your place."

They glared at each other, the tension heavy in the silence surrounding us. It was Cal who broke it first. "I remember it all, Newt. Every single thing. About me. And about you."

Uncle Newt flushed and for an instant, I saw a flash of something that frightened me cross his face. There and gone. It happened so fast, I wondered if I'd imagined it. His words were firm and even as he responded. "I'll pass your concerns on to Angus, but don't expect him to change his mind about this. You know how he can be." With that, Uncle Newt left, the sudden pressure change as he returned Below making my ears hurt until they popped.

Cal was staring at where Newt had been a second before and I heard him whisper one final thing. "Coward."

"Hells, Cal, what was that about?" He looked so angry I didn't dare cross the distance between us. Still, I needed to know.

He took a deep breath, the tension in him seeming to ease as he exhaled. "Ancient history, Laney. I'm sorry you were involved in that."

"What do you mean, ancient history?"

Cal looked at me, his eyes deep and fathomless. He opened his mouth to speak, but we were interrupted.

"What'd I miss?" Torren asked, entering the kitchen. He looked rested, better than he had when he'd shown up at the crack of dawn. His hair was mussed from sleep but the shadows under his eyes had faded slightly. He'd lost the hunched appearance he'd had earlier. The marked difference was hard to miss.

I watched as Cal's face closed down, his guard sliding back into place. "Nothing," he said, turning to Tor. "A difference of opinion with an old friend, that's all. Better get something to eat, man. I'll meet you downstairs. You need to get back to training. Laney's way ahead of you now." Then he headed back downstairs to the basement, Moose following behind him.

"You all right, Laney?" Tor asked.

I nodded. "Yeah. A little tired, I guess. Sparring with him never seems to get any easier."

"Didn't seem like nothing," he said.

The shift in conversation caught me off guard for a moment. "Huh?"

"Whatever was going on in here." He held up his hands as I narrowed my eyes at him. "Hey, I wasn't trying to eavesdrop. I was coming down to get some food after waking up. Heard the conversation all the way out in the living room. Thought it might be a good idea to wait until some of the tension eased a little bit before I showed myself."

I had to give him some credit for recognizing that walking into a battle of wills between Newt and Cal was probably not the best thing to do. Especially with him having just returned to the house.

"Is it true, what Cal said?" Torren's voice shifted to a softer, more worried tone. "That you almost died last night?"

I shrugged. "Cal doesn't lie. If he said I almost died, I'm pretty sure I almost died. Of course, I was unconscious for most of it. So, I have that to be thankful for at least."

He walked past me to the refrigerator, his eyes not meeting mine. "He healed you, then." There was discomfort there, which I assumed was linked to the knowledge of how Cal's ability to heal worked. Heat and skin-to-skin contact allowed for the best results.

I nodded. "He did. Feeling pretty good overall. I might take a nap though, while you guys get reacquainted."

He chuckled at that. "I'm sure Cal can't wait to get his hands on me. Better get down there and take my punishment." He opened the basement door, the one Callum had shut very firmly a few minutes before. Before he descended the stairs, he looked at me, his eyes locking with mine. "I want you to know, well, I'm really happy to be home, Laney."

I didn't say anything, unsure how I was feeling about all that had happened. Tor gave me a sad smile and shut the door behind him.

Chapter Thirteen

MUCH LIKE WHEN Torren first joined our little household, we soon fell into a rhythm that allowed us to live side by side without killing each other. I didn't see what happened between Cal and Tor during that workout and Moose didn't share their secrets with me. All I can say is they both came out of it alive and breathing. They didn't talk about it. Tor ended up with an impressive black eye and Cal walked away with a painfully swollen split lip. They both carried their injuries with an air of pride, making me curious about exactly what had transpired during their sparring session. They seemed to have worked something out that kept the animosity at bay, softening the sharp edges that had surrounded them both when Torren came back.

The men established a truce, of sorts. There were times when I'd find them sitting at the table in the kitchen, discussing the security we had in place or even plans for how we would approach another assignment from Angus. If that ever came. Since Uncle Newt's last visit, we hadn't heard anything. Cal was on edge, openly wondering about the silence. Torren suggested that maybe Angus had taken Cal's message to heart and was rethinking his decision to involve me in the troubles brewing Below. I wisely stayed out of those conversations. I didn't want to tempt fate. They were getting along, which was all I could hope for.

Torren was also learning how to manage his emotions better around me. I was no longer overwhelmed with the sudden influx of his feelings. Without the distraction of Tor's emotions interfering during a battle, we were able to work together again. Cal finally agreed to train us both at the same time after seeing how much we had improved. We were learning to work together as a team. Moose even got pulled into the fray a few times. He and Cal fought together seamlessly when they needed to, anticipating each other's next steps as they moved. This was what Cal wanted us all to be able to do. To fight beside each other as a unit. We'd be stronger together than trying to battle our enemies separately.

Callum was relentless, and it was paying off. I might have been sore and bruised more often than not, but we were getting better. His training was working. My father had been right in assigning him this role. Cal was tough, but he knew what he was doing. After a few days, Torren and I were able to fight side by side, my magic complementing his own fighting skills and the weapons training he'd had.

As we finished a session, sweat dripping from both of us, he gave me a tired grin. "You need more target practice. Your aim is off. A little high and to the left."

I holstered my Witness and pulled a knife from its sheath on my thigh. I flipped the knife end over end, catching it as I spun. My arm arced forward, and I released the knife. It hit the target square in the chest with a dull thud. "I think I'm doing perfectly fine." I winked at him and headed upstairs, a new swagger in my walk. Torren's laugh as I left him behind made me smile. Things were definitely looking up.

I COULD FEEL MYSELF growing stronger. Physically, the constant workouts Callum put us through were paying off. I'd thought I was in shape before he came to live here. I was so wrong. He'd taken everything I'd done to a higher level and I was able to see the results each time I looked in the mirror. The soft curves I'd had were being replaced, strength evident in the gentle swell of lean muscle on my arms and legs. My core had tightened, becoming a firmer foundation supporting my every move. I even caught myself standing differently as I adapted to this new version of me. Pride swelled as I examined the woman reflected back at me. She was becoming a warrior.

More so than the physical changes I could see, I knew the biggest change had come in how I was able to control my magic. I had a confidence now that I'd never had before.

When I sparred with Cal, the magic was a natural addition to what we were doing, and I'd earned a few compliments on how much I'd improved. I knew he wasn't going to let me go running off after demons on my own, even if I was stronger than before. The difference was, I didn't want to fight those battles alone anymore. We were a team. If there was a fight to be had, we were going to fight it together.

Chapter Fourteen

When I came downstairs the next morning, my hair still wet from a quick shower, I was surprised to find Torren alone in the kitchen. He was hunched over the kitchen table, a pen scratching across paper. I hesitated. Nerves erupted, my stomach rolling for a moment at the sight of him. Tor and I hadn't been alone since he'd returned. Cal and Moose had always provided a buffer with their presence.

"Might as well come on in." Torren twisted as he looked over his shoulder at me, then returned to what he'd been writing. "It's not like I couldn't hear you coming down the stairs. You're not exactly stealthy."

The teasing tone in his voice made me grin. If there was one thing Cal complained about the most, it was how heavily I walked. At this point, he'd almost given up commenting on it.

I clomped my way over to the refrigerator, pulling open

the door so hard, the items inside rattled. Torren laughed and I joined in as I pulled a pitcher of tea off the shelf. I kicked the door shut behind me and then, really getting into the spirit of the moment, stomped over to the counter.

"Pretty sure that's exactly the technique Cal would suggest you use. You know, when you're sneaking up on a demon."

I nodded, playing along. "What can I say, I'm the best student he's ever had."

Torren laughed loudly, his paper forgotten. "I'm sure. The very best."

The basement door opened, Callum appearing as if simply speaking his name had been magic. I hadn't heard him coming up the wooden stairs at all. But then again, we hadn't been exactly quiet.

"What're the two of you doing up here? It sounds like a herd of buffalo stampeding. I thought the floor was going to collapse."

"Oh, you know. Laney was practicing her sneaky walk." Torren laughed again. "I think she might finally be improving."

I gasped and grinned at them both, pouring my tea into a glass. "Don't know what you two are talking about. I'm the quiet one in this group."

That earned a chuckle from Cal. I soaked in the relaxed atmosphere spreading through the room. Inspiration struck.

"Hey guys, why don't we all go get some food. In Hazelwood." The diner in town was known for the best home cooking around. Callum had a particular favorite there.

"Apple pie?" he asked, giving me one of his real smiles. I hadn't seen that since Torren's return. It made me happy to see it back, even if it was only because of the possibility of dessert.

"As much as Anita will let you have," I promised. There was something adorable about how much Callum loved that pie. "But you better grab Moose. He'll never forgive us if you get to have apple pie and he doesn't."

He nodded at me. "Give me five minutes. Then we're out of here."

He ran out the back door, yelling Moose's name, excitement in his voice.

"Wow, I'd never have guessed his weakness was apple pie."

I winked at him. "Wait until you see how much he eats, then let me know if you think it's actually a weakness."

Chapter Fifteen

THE DRIVE TO Hazelwood was a nice respite from our secluded routine. It was a cold, clear day, the fields lining the highway covered in snow that glittered in the sunlight. I tuned out the conversation between Cal and Tor, enjoying the relaxed feeling driving always gave me. My mind wandered, and I found myself thinking about the group of demons we'd encountered when Newt had sent us on the assignment from Angus. So many demons concentrated in one place was unusual, especially when they were mixed like that. Demons usually only associated with their own kind and didn't interact with others often. It would take something of significant importance for them to come together.

The edge of Hazelwood appeared, the stones marking the town's boundaries dark against the white snow surrounding them. I slowed at the sight of them. For most people, they were nothing more than a lovely bit of landscaping, welcoming people into Hazelwood. But for those who understood their importance, the stones were a beacon. They warded the town, keeping residents safe. The magic within them was centuries old. Miss Tilly kept the power fresh, her own magic layered into the rock, combining with what had come before. I knew from previous experience that evil couldn't cross over the barrier they created. The stones were simply too strong.

Familiarity directed my every movement of the steering wheel. As I pulled up in front of the shining windows of The Hedgerow, Cal shot me a questioning look.

"I thought we were coming for pie?"

I shrugged. "I should probably stop in and see Miss Tilly. It's the polite thing to do. And we all know how much Miss Tilly appreciates politeness."

Cal nodded in response as he opened his door. "No doubt she'd find out we're in town before the pie even made it to the table. I'm hungry, but I'm not willing to risk missing out on that pie. Torren and I can walk Moose around out here while you visit."

Torren didn't argue. He and Miss Tilly weren't on the best of terms. She thought he was rude. He thought she was strange. It was going to be a while before they could work things out. I watched them walk away down the street, Moose pulling them along. When they turned the corner, I left my car and walked into Miss Tilly's store.

The bell above the front door rang out, a loud, clear

sound. There was no one I could see inside, but I could feel Miss Tilly's presence. She was here. I needed to be patient.

I looked over the amulets resting on velvet inside a glass display case. A few were large, with polished stones that soaked up the light. I was drawn more to the smaller ones. They seemed to radiate joy and serenity.

The sound of a door closing pulled my head up. Miss Tilly made her way over to where I stood by the front counter, her steps quiet. "Hello, Girl. Good of you to come see me."

In the time since we'd first met, she'd never called me by my name. I didn't understand why, but at the same time, I didn't question her about it. It was simply her way.

I pointed to the amulets in the case. "These are very nice. Are they new?"

Miss Tilly nodded. "Aften's practice. She needs to learn many things still. But she's improving. These will be useful to those they are meant for."

"This purple one is beautiful," I said, tapping the glass above the amulet. The stone set within the shining silver circle sparkled in response and I had the sudden urge to hold it in my hand. "Can I see it more closely?"

"That one is not for you." The sharp tone in her voice surprised me, pulling my head up. Miss Tilly's eyes were intent on me, and I took a step back involuntarily. Miss Tilly sighed, and I wondered at how relieved she sounded. "It is intended for someone else. Someone who needs it."

I held my hands out, feeling the need for her to see that

they were empty. I tried to steer the conversation to a safer topic. "I understand. How long will it be before Aften takes over for you?"

"No one can tell. It all depends on the person. When she is ready, then it will be time. Until then, I will wait." She came around the counter to me, the rings on her fingers sparking as the light shifted around her. "It is good you are here. There are storms coming. You should know to be ready for them."

She walked to the front door and I followed, pulled along by the power of her presence. "Storms? What kind of storms?" I was certain these wouldn't be garden variety thunderstorms, not if she was bringing them up.

"I've seen darkness." She paused, her hand hovering above the handle of the door. "Aften has as well. Others come to us with their visions of it. It has become a larger concern. We are preparing. You will as well." She pulled the door open for me and the bell rang again, harsher and less welcoming this time. Cal and Torren were waiting for me in the sunlight, leaning against my car as they chatted. Moose was laying at their feet. "Go now, Girl. Join your men. Time is short."

Before I understood what was happening, I was standing on the sidewalk, the shop door closing behind me. Miss Tilly said one final thing before the door clicked shut. "I'm sorry for your pain," was all I heard before she was gone, and the lights inside went off. I looked back, searching for some sign of movement through the windows, but there was nothing.

"Laney, you alright?"

Cal's voice pulled my attention back to our original reason for coming to town. Pie. "Yeah," I said, giving him a small smile. "Fine. Just some things Miss Tilly said. I'll have to think about them a bit. You know how she can be."

Torren chuckled. "More cryptic warnings? Or did she chastise you for not coming to see her sooner?"

I shook my head. "Not today." That was strange. Normally, Miss Tilly felt the need to point out that I was late according to whatever timetable she had running in her head. I didn't question her knowledge. If she said I was late for something, I probably was. But the change did make me wonder.

Cal reached a hand toward me and I took it, letting him pull me forward. "Let's go. Moose is dying for the pie we promised him."

I didn't protest as we walked away from The Hedgerow. This was supposed to be our break from the worry and hard work. The guys talked happily as we made our way across the street.

The bright green door of Hazelwood's diner opened, a group of people stepping out onto the sidewalk. Their laughter made me smile, the happiness from them driving away some of the worry simmering in me after talking with Miss Tilly.

I glanced down at Moose. He'd shifted into his Yorkie

form before we left the house. Standing on the street outside the diner, he tipped his head to the side, like he was asking me what we were waiting for. He looked like any other dog, the purple leash clipped to his collar acting as his own kind of bright camouflage.

"You'll really do anything for Anita's apple pie, won't you?" I whispered to him as I reached down to pet his head. He panted at me, then swiped his tongue across my hand. That was an unconditional yes.

"Will she let him in?" Torren asked as we stepped up to the door, Moose trotting along beside me.

I shook my head. "No idea. But this time, we're going to ask for her permission, not sneak him in." I shot a pointed glance at Callum, who grinned at the look.

"We learned our lesson last time. I promise." He held the door open for me, taking Moose's leash in his hand. Moose dropped down into a sit immediately, looking like we'd trained him to do it. "We'll wait out here while you sweet talk Anita for us. We're not willing to risk missing out on pie."

I couldn't help but laugh at that. "I'll do my best, guys. Back in minute. Wish me luck."

I heard Cal say, "Good luck," before the door shut. Torren and I entered the diner. Most of the tables were occupied so I pointed him in the direction of an open booth.

"Go ahead and have a seat at that table down there. I'll find Anita and see what we can work out."

Tor went to claim our booth and I made my way to the front counter. All the stools were taken, men and women from Hazelwood sipping coffee as they ate. Gossip and laughter flew, the mood light as it usually was inside the Green Door. I waited patiently next to the counter until a waitress walked by. I caught her attention, asking her to let the owner know I needed a moment of her time.

She gave me an understanding nod and then disappeared into the back through a swinging door. Everything else continued around me, the diner in constant motion as people came and went. The space was warm and friendly, almost like you were being welcomed home. It was always this way. It was the magic of the Green Door Diner. It made you want to come back.

"Well, look who it is." The voice coming from behind me was a surprise. I'd been so focused on everyone else, I'd missed Anita coming out into the front of the restaurant. "Apple pie, I'm assuming?"

I gave her a small smile. "Absolutely. Maybe a few sandwiches too, but definitely apple pie."

She leaned to her left, looking around me. "Where's your man? And the dog?"

I pointed to the door. "Cal's waiting outside, with Moose. We didn't want to bring him in without asking you first. My friend Torren is sitting at the booth over there." I pointed at him and he waved back at us. We were pouring on the friendly gestures today. "If it's okay with you, Moose can lay on the floor under the table. We'll make sure he's not in the way." I thought back to the first time Callum and Moose had indulged in her apple pie. Somehow, Moose had managed to sneak his way in and joined Cal at a table. I was pretty sure magic had been involved on that occasion. This time around, we were going to do this like anyone else would.

She gave me a direct look, her eyes bright behind the lenses of the glasses she wore. "He stays under the table. And only one piece of pie. For each of you."

I smiled. "Thank you, Anita. I promise, we'll make sure he's out of the way. You won't regret this."

I didn't give her a chance to say anything else. I slipped out the door to where Cal and Moose were waiting outside. The hopeful look in Moose's eyes was adorable. Cal's wasn't far behind.

"We're in." I leaned down, scratching Moose under the chin. "You have to stay under our table while we're in there. And only one piece of pie."

I stood up and led them both to the door, holding it open so they could walk through.

"One piece?" Cal asked, frowning. "Only one?"

"For each of us." I said. When that didn't cheer him up, I added, "Oh, go on. You can have mine too."

He grinned in response and headed inside. Moose's stubby tail twitched happily as he followed. The sight of them so easily pleased made me smile. They were proof that sometimes things could be very simple. And we needed a good dose of simple.

Chapter Sixteen

That happiness carried us through the night. During the drive home, Torren and Cal traded jokes with each other. Moose, back in his sleek Hound form, barked a laugh at the particularly funny ones. It reminded me of the last birthday party my mom had thrown for me when Angus was still able to live with us Above. He and Newt had traded jokes rapid fire, back and forth, until Mom and I were begging them to stop because our stomachs hurt from laughing so hard. She'd threatened to not let them have any cake if they didn't give us a chance to catch our breath. I smiled at the memory. My mom always made the best cake and they took her warning to heart. There were big slices of Devil's Food for each of us that day, although I'm pretty sure my dad was sneaky and stole an extra one when no one was looking. It had been a good day.

After I parked in the garage, we chose to avoid the cold

by using the tunnel that ran from the garage into the basement of the house. Moose led the way, sniffing at every corner and growling at spiders that ran away at our approach. We were all laughing together as we climbed the stairs, spilling out into the kitchen where Uncle Newt was waiting for us, sitting at the table, a glass of smoky amber liquid in front of him.

I froze, surprised to find him alone in the dark of my home. He had a strange look on his face, as if he was angry we weren't here when he'd arrived. Cal came to a quick stop behind me, stumbling when Torren ran into him. Guilt flared through me, unexpectedly. What did I have to feel guilty about? We'd been out, enjoying our time together. There was nothing wrong with that.

"Did you all have fun? Playing instead of preparing?" The question dripped with disdain. It was clear he didn't really expect an answer.

I felt Cal straighten behind me, but I placed my hand on his chest. I would handle this.

"We've been working hard and needed a little time away. Blow some stink off and relax. I'm assuming you're here because you need us to do something for you. Or for Angus."

He nodded, holding the glass up and swirling his drink around before raising it to his lips. He shot me a glance over the rim, his eyes cold as he watched me. He sipped the liquid and the scent of alcohol steeped with cinnamon reached me.

He was drinking my whiskey. The gift from my father. It shouldn't have bothered me, I never drank it. But it was something Angus had given me. A moment between us, as he'd laughed at the dancing devil on the outside of the bottle and I'd rolled my eyes. It was special to me.

"Angus has a job for you. Another chance. Try not to burn the place to the ground this time." He pulled a folded piece of paper from the pocket of the jacket he wore, tossing it down onto the table as he stood and drained the remaining whiskey in the glass.

My irritation was replaced by unease. Something was off. I'd never seen my father's best friend act this way. "Uncle Newt, what's wrong?" I asked, reaching out to grab his wrist as he turned to go. "This isn't like you."

He looked down at where my fingers rested against his skin, shaking his head. "Things are falling apart, Delaney, more than you know. And you weren't here, working to prepare yourself for what you'll need to do."

"She can't train constantly, Newton." Cal said, his protectiveness spiking. "She needs a break from time to time. She's earned it. We all have."

Newt's eyes flickered between us, taking in the way Cal had angled himself in front of me and Torren moved into position on my left side. Moose was silent, slinking up beside Cal. We were a team.

"I hope you're right, Callum. Because you're all going to be tested. Soon."

He tossed the glass up into the air and stepped back, falling into a portal that opened and closed so quickly that he was gone before the glass began its descent. Cal reached out and snagged it, keeping it from smashing against the wood planks.

"That was weird." Torren's comment broke the tension and a nervous laugh left me.

"It was." Cal carefully set the glass on the table, then turned to face us. "Not like Newton at all to act that way."

"Things must really be worse than I realized if he's that upset we took a little time off to relax. He was always encouraging me not to work so hard before." I stared at the space where my father's best friend had just disappeared, thoughts whirling as I tried to understand his abrupt change in attitude.

Cal picked up the paper Uncle Newt had left behind, reviewing the writing on it before handing it to me. I glanced over it, my breath catching.

Cal grimaced as he caught my eye. "Better get ready. We leave in an hour."

Chapter Seventeen

It was hard to believe that a few hours earlier, we were seated around a table, laughing as we indulged ourselves with the best apple pie any of us had ever tasted. I'd come to understand, as Anita had lingered at our booth off and on while we ate, that this was her particular brand of magic. She could blend the individual ingredients into a new whole, infusing it with more than flavor. Her food was filled with love. Gruff though she might appear, she cared for all who came into the Green Door. She created a haven for people who needed to leave the world behind for a short time. It seemed simple, but it was much more complex than I'd ever realized.

The thought of the fun we'd had together made crouching on the cold ground a little less horrible. Even wearing multiple layers, I was shivering as the cold relentlessly wormed its way into my bones. My toes were numb, my fingers aching inside the gloves I wore. I tried to keep myself still and silent but could no longer hold the shivers at bay. Moose pressed his full length to my side, lending me his warmth, and I greedily soaked it in.

Cal crept back to where Moose and I waited. He gestured back the way he'd come. Keeping his voice low, barely above a whisper, he said, "They're here, exactly as Newton told us they'd be. Torren's watching them for now."

"How many?" I asked, my teeth no longer chattering.

"Fewer than the first time."

I narrowed my eyes at him, knowing from experience he'd have no trouble seeing my expression in the dark. "What are they doing here?"

He shrugged. "It looks like they're waiting for something. Or someone. Come on."

Moose and I followed Cal as he turned, choosing our path carefully to pass as silently as possibly. We were under the cover of trees, so there was less snow on the ground here. We'd used a portal to bring us close to the location listed on Uncle Newt's note, then had walked the rest of the way, hoping to have the advantage of surprise.

I kept one hand on Moose's back as we made our way forward. He was steady and strong. Like before, I knew he wouldn't leave me, even if I tried to send him away. He'd claimed me long before I realized I'd made him mine. He twisted his head, nudging my leg, and I understood the unspoken message easily enough. We would take care of each other, as we always did.

Nervousness flared in my stomach for a moment as I settled beside Cal and Torren. I looked to where Cal directed me, taking in the sight of a small fire in a clearing up ahead. The light danced across the faces of demons clustered together. Their voices were raised as they argued with each other.

Once again, I was surprised to find the various species of demons in one place. Demons typically preferred to be on their own and when they had to join forces, they were almost always found gathered with their own kind. This marked two occasions where we'd found them mixing with each other. Although based on what we were hearing, it didn't appear they were getting along very well this time.

"What are they waiting for?" Torren whispered.

Cal leaned in, keeping his voice low as well. "I think it's who they're waiting for we need to be worried about. Not what."

I tuned the two men out, instead focusing on the group of demons who continued to argue. The voices in the clearing were getting louder, the tension in the group ratcheting up. I heard snatches of the debate, but one thing caught my attention. My name, shouted from somewhere in the middle of the group, was audible. The response was angry.

I wondered what this group of demons was doing here.

Uncle Newt had described these rogue groups of demons as unhappy with my father's leadership Below. Challengers to his throne. The discord playing out in front of us certainly didn't indicate a united front.

A rolling bark echoed from the clearing in front of us. Moose stiffened beside me, a barely audible growl vibrating from him. The voices in the clearing paused, as if waiting for some signal. Silence rang out, and I froze in place, holding my breath. A howl shattered the quiet and the group was instantly moving, swinging around to where we crouched in the shadows. Another howl rang out, joined by others, until it was a chorus. They had Hounds with them, circling the area, standing sentry. We had been scented. They were coming for us.

Chapter Eighteen

Cal cursed under his breath and Moose growled low. Cal's hand landed on my shoulder. "Stay here." Before I could respond, he and Moose were gone, sliding into the shadows and disappearing.

Torren crouched on the ground next to me. I felt a spark of fear through the connection between us and reached for his hand. He squeezed my hand in return and then released it. Both of us immediately drew our weapons. I quieted my breathing, forcing myself to slow down, counting the spaces between inhale and exhale. I needed to be steady.

I whispered to Torren. "Cal wouldn't have left if he thought we needed him. They'll be back."

Tor grunted, his only response. Even though we'd been working together, even though I felt our relationship was stronger than before, there was no denying that Torren and

Callum weren't the best of friends. He didn't have the same trust in Cal that I did. Not yet.

I heard a rustling to our left and twisted toward it, careful to move as soundlessly as possible. The group that had gathered in the clearing had dispersed, the flames dying down. Torren's presence at my side was familiar. He would watch my back. Of that I had no doubt.

Closing my eyes, I pulled my magic up. Callum had been drilling me during our training sessions, forcing me to use my power against him. He wanted me to be ready for anything that might come at us. Weapons and fighting skill might not be enough. I'd learned that having magic ready and waiting was better than reaching for it at the last second, when everything else was falling apart. A grim smile crept across my face as I realized how much I'd changed since Cal and I had met.

"That's a scary grin," whispered Torren, his voice barely audible.

"Just thinking about things," I said. "You ready?"

I felt him move next to me, as if preparing himself to spring forward. "As I'll ever be."

The brush in front of us parted and four figures stalked out, heading straight toward our hiding place. My breathing began to speed up at the sight of them, but I forced it to slow, returning to a regular, measured rhythm. My pulse quieted and my hands stopped shaking. I raised my gun and sighted at my first target, the largest of the bunch. The air beside me moved and I knew Torren was locked in as well. I let my breath out slowly as my finger lingered on the trigger, ready to take the shot.

The cracking of limbs sounded in the trees and the group stopped, their attention turning to where the sound had come from. I didn't breathe, not wanting even the slightest exhale to snag their focus. The largest of the four stepped toward the noise, the other three aligning themselves behind them, fists clenched and ready. The buzz of electricity tickled across my skin and I knew they were arming themselves with their own magic.

Callum stepped out from the shadows, Moose at his side. I flinched in surprise at seeing the two of them there, in the line of danger, but I didn't dare move yet. Somewhere inside me, I understood, the timing wasn't right. I trusted Cal knew what he was doing.

"Cain," he said, no warmth in his voice. Not a friendly greeting. "Imagine my surprise finding you here."

"Imagine my lack of surprise at seeing you, then." Cain's words were snarky, sarcasm dripping from them. "Always the lackey, doing as he's told."

I wanted to rush out from where I was hidden, wanted to defend my friend. Torren's hand settled on my shoulder, reassuring me even as it held me in place.

Cal didn't seem bothered by the intended insult. "Not doing as I was told is what got me sent here. Same as you."

"But now you're his assassin. Killing those who would go

a different way. Another faithful dog, aren't you? Except you can't shift." He pointed to where Moose stood, and even from where I waited, I couldn't miss the growl that vibrated from my Hound.

"I'm trying to keep the peace, Cain. That's all. If there weren't demons threatening it, we wouldn't be here."

Cain laughed, the sound almost a bark in the night. The three with him joined in and I reined in the urge to jump out at them, to punish them for the way they taunted my friends.

"Peace?" asked Cain, looking back at his friends. "All we've ever wanted is what we were promised. We've bled for that. Now, we're willing to fight for what we're owed. Even if you're the one standing in our way tonight."

I gasped silently as the other demons we'd seen before filtered in to join the four Cal had been talking with. I didn't see the Hounds we'd heard, but I was sure they were still out there.

Callum and Moose sank into what I recognized were their fighting stances. Cal didn't draw his sword, but I knew it was only a thought away. My heart began to race, the heavy beat of my pulse loud in my head, and I worried that the demons would hear it. Torren's hand on my shoulder tightened and the bond between us thrummed, reminding me he was there.

Cain laughed again, the rest of the group joining in as they assessed Callum and Moose. Then Cain leaned in, close enough he could've tapped Cal on the chest if he'd been brave enough, and said, "Give her to us, Callum. We'll let you go and make sure to kill her quickly. Our gift to you."

It was Cal who growled this time, fury radiating from him, and there was a pulse of energy that surged out of him. The impact as it collided with the bodies of the demons before him was shocking, the sound of bones cracking ringing out in the night. Screams of pain rose up, high and panicked. Cain somehow managed to hold his ground against that force as it tore into those around him. Swearing in a language I didn't recognize, he launched himself forward. Cal sidestepped, letting Cain's momentum carry him too far. Then his sword was in his hand, flames racing along the blade as it arced down and slashed into the meat of Cain's back.

Moose howled, jumping into the fight as those demons still standing sought to join in. Cal gave a nod to where Torren and I waited. Our signal. Gathering ourselves, we jumped up and left our small shelter. My weapon was up, magic ready, as we emerged at the rear of the group, taking them all by surprise.

The ones who spun to face us were the first to fall, the blessed bullets quick and efficient. I set a shield around us, allowing me and Tor to push forward into the midst of the rebel demons. Any that threatened to breach my barrier, I used a purifying spell on, the magic burning them from the inside out. I forced myself to ignore their screams and move on to the next target, but nausea swirled in my stomach.

Slowly the opposition's advantage was eaten away, Moose and Callum relentless from their position at the front. Torren and I were in the rear, working together to keep any of the rogues from escaping. I could feel my energy waver, the drain of holding the shield in place around us as we fought beginning to weigh on me. Cal's constant drills had built my strength, increased my stamina, but I was fading.

I shouted to Torren, a warning so he'd be ready. His gaze twisted to me, understanding on his face as he nodded. He reloaded, raised his guns, and I dropped the shield that surrounded us.

The noise that rushed in as the barrier dropped was disorienting, and it took me a moment to adjust. That one moment was all it took for two demons, a Siren and a Chaos as far as I could tell, to hurl themselves toward me.

I let loose the purifying fire on them both, but this time there was nothing to dull their screams as they were devoured. Bile filled my throat and I gagged before swallowing it back down. I'd fought and killed before when necessary, to protect myself and others. Something about this felt different. I made myself watch them die, their agony as they were consumed. When they were piles of ash at my feet, I pressed on to where Torren was struggling with a demon on the ground.

I pulled my knife from my boot, the blessed blade gleaming bright and jammed it into the back of the demon pinning

Tor. The demon roared, twisting toward me, eyes going wide as if he recognized me, his hand reaching for my chest as Torren's gun barked. The demon flinched as the bullet entered, dark blood bubbling at the edge of his mouth before his eyes closed.

Torren took the hand I offered him, and we were up, fighting again. We worked in tandem, our movements sure and confident, knowing exactly where the other person was as the bond between the two of us broadcast constantly. We didn't need to talk in these moments. It was a freeing feeling as we trusted that connection to steer us through the battle.

I knocked the demon in front of me to the ground, his eyes rolling up as I followed my strike by plunging my knife into his gut. Sweat dripped down my face and my hand came away sticky as I wiped it away. I spun, searching out Callum and Moose. Relief rose in my chest as I saw them taking down the last few demons that remained. I took a step toward them but stumbled as a hand wrapped around my ankle. One of the rebels, already injured, had grabbed for me as I passed by. Claws bit down, breaking skin and I yelped as I fell, momentum carrying me down to the ground. I twisted, wrenching my leg free as I staggered to my knees. My knife was in my hand, ready to fall, when the rogue held its hands out, a pleading gesture.

"Wait, please," it whispered. "Help me."

I froze, my hand hovering above it, and I couldn't bring myself to finish the blow. I sagged down, the energy fueling me moments ago suddenly gone. The demon reached out, retracting its claws. As I leaned toward it, there was an explosion next to the left side of my head, heat searing my cheek. I fell off to the side, shocked and hurt, viscous fluid coating me. I sucked in air as I was hauled up to my feet, Torren's furious face suddenly in front of me.

"Never hesitate. Never again." He spat the words, pulling me along with him as he pressed forward to where Cal and Moose stood over the fallen Cain.

Callum looked me over, worry flitting across his face, before he forced it back to nothingness. He turned his attention back to Cain, who was no longer laughing.

"Tell me now. Tell me and I promise, it will be over." The command in Cal's voice was unmistakable. He was powerful, and I knew Cain wouldn't be able to refuse.

"They're coming for her. She's the key." The words poured from Cain, pain running through them. "And the other soul as well. Once they have them both, all Below will be theirs for the taking." He rolled to his side, coughing blood into the dirt.

"Who's coming? Where are they?" asked Callum, his power demanding more.

Cain's body flinched, as if the questions were physical blows. "I don't know any more. They haven't told us." He choked, anything else he might have said lost as he struggled to breathe around the blood in his throat.

Moose barked, circling around to stand beside me. I saw

the unmoving bodies of the other Hounds, the ones we'd heard and hadn't been able to see. I rested my hand on Moose's head, wondering at how hard it must've been for him to kill his own kind.

Cal's sword flared bright as it swung down, severing Cain's head from his body. Quick, exactly as he'd promised. I watched as Cal rested, his weight leaning on the sword as it was buried in the soil, exhaustion heavy on him. I gave him a moment to gather himself, to process the act of killing this being he'd known. When I crossed the gap between us, reaching out to him, he took my hand and stood. He whispered something low, the power of it charging the air around me and his sword disappeared, returning to wherever it waited for his call.

"We need to clean this up as best we can," he said, surveying the mess. There were bodies spread out on the ground, those I hadn't already burned to cinders.

I nodded in understanding. "We'll gather them up, into a pile. Then I'll purify them. Erase all traces. Torren and I can handle that. You rest for a bit."

He didn't argue with me. Torren and I pulled the bodies into the center of the battlefield, Moose dragging some over as well. When we had them all together, I tapped into my remaining energy reserves. The smell of ozone rose in the air as my magic surged, and I burned all that was left to ash.

Cal's eyes were full of compassion as we limped to where he waited for us. I didn't like killing and he knew it. His fingers found mine, squeezing them tightly in reassurance, reminding me he was there. Then he opened a portal for us to make our way home.

Chapter Nineteen

That battle seemed to solidify something between us. We'd worked together, as a team, protecting each other even if we didn't always get along. The men sniped at each other less. Callum didn't take it any easier on us as we trained. In fact, it almost felt like he pushed harder than he had before. As if he'd seen something he was determined to improve upon.

After another grueling session, I staggered up the stairs to the kitchen and fell into a chair. A glass of water and a protein shake appeared almost magically in front of me. I could barely lift my head to look at the man who'd put them there.

"You're going to kill us." I growled at him, my vocal cords the only muscles I still had any control over.

He grinned and shook his head. "Actually, I'm going to keep you from getting killed. Now, drink. You need the extra protein. And hydration. We're building muscle, you know."

I stuck my tongue out at him, thankful to find I could still use that as well. He winked at me and headed back downstairs, probably to continue torturing Torren and Moose. My stomach started to rumble, unhappy with how empty it was after all that work. I waited until Cal's footsteps had faded before I lifted the protein shake to my lips and took a sip. Then downed the rest without taking a breath.

I grumbled under my breath as I rested my head on the table. "Devil save me from those who want to protect me."

Cal's voice carried up through the floorboards at my feet. "I heard that. I'm beginning to rethink letting you take a break."

His laughter followed me as I left the kitchen as fast as my aching legs could carry me to my room. All I wanted was a hot shower and a nap.

Chapter Twenty

I WALKED THE perimeter of the property, snow crunching under my feet as I took my turn checking our defenses. The wards still vibrated warmly from the ground beneath my feet as I started off. The steady rhythm reassured me. They shouldn't need charging for a while. Cal's work to extend our security had paid off. When we had time, I'd ask him to show me how he'd done that. His knowledge was vast, and I was willing to learn whatever he would teach.

The air around me seemed to coalesce abruptly and Moose gave a yip, racing back to my side and immediately shifting from his Yorkie form into the sleek black Hell Hound he truly was. When my father appeared, stepping out of the trees and brush onto the cleared ground in front of me, Moose gave a happy bark and twitched his tail back and forth.

"Hound," Angus said gravely, as Moose put his paws out

and stretched, his muzzle down. It was a dignified canine type of bow. "I'm pleased to see you as well."

I waited as Moose was given a few pats on the head and then my father produced a stick from the empty air beside him. He held it out and Moose went instantly still, his eyes intent on the prize waiting for him. Angus smiled and then spun, throwing the stick out into the air. "Go get it."

Moose jumped forward and raced after the toy that soared through the cold air. My father gave a chuckle as he watched my Hound chase after the airborne object.

"Hey Dad," I said as Angus turned to me. He gently pulled me into a hug, his lips brushing across my forehead. As always, heat radiated from him and chased the cold away. "When did you teach him to play fetch?"

Angus put his arm around me, the worn leather jacket he constantly wore soft and comfortingly familiar. The spicy scent of brimstone followed him everywhere and, as he held me close, I breathed it in. The smell of it had the power to return me to the little girl I'd been years ago. Tension I hadn't realized I'd been carrying eased from my shoulders as I wrapped my arms around him. His steady presence brought a smile to my face.

"I didn't teach him this game. We can blame Callum for that, I believe. But he enjoys it and I don't mind indulging him. He's a good dog. Most days."

We walked along and he asked the question I'd been dreading. "How are things now? At home?"

I shrugged and leaned into the warmth he radiated a little more. "They're dealing with each other. Did you know Torren left us for a while?"

"It was mentioned." He didn't elaborate and I didn't pry.

"Things were easier, in a way, when he was gone. Cal and Moose were definitely more relaxed. But I worried about him."

"And now?"

"There's still tension, though it's getting better. Tor's trying. He seems less angry, but I can't tell if that's because he's resigned himself to this situation or it's something else. I worry that he's given up." I waited, hoping my father would offer some good advice, or better yet, a solution to the whole problem itself. We'd all been hoping to discover some way to dissolve the magical bond that tied Torren to me. When my dad didn't say anything, I prodded him. "Well, what do you think?"

Angus stopped walking and turned to face me. "Delaney, I'm your father. My only concern in this business is how that man can be of use to you. That's all I care about." As I started to protest, he stopped me with a shake of his head. "If I had my way, you'd have less of these principles you cling so tightly to and more self-preservation instincts."

He gripped my hands in his and looked down at them, his large fingers wrapping around my smaller ones which had begun to shake, chilled through. I'd forgotten gloves when

I came outside. With a grin, because he knew how much I hated the cold, he amplified the warmth leaking from him. His grip on my fingers tightened and the heat soaked into me. The pain and stiffness eased. "But then, you wouldn't be you, and I can't stand the thought of that either. So here we are."

I nodded, understanding his point. We stood like that for a moment longer, before Moose rushed up to us, the stick he'd been chasing firmly held in his teeth.

I gave him a few well-earned scratches behind his perked-up ears. "Good boy, Moosie." He gave me an affectionate nudge in return and then carefully placed the stick at my father's feet, dropping to his haunches to sit at attention. I could sense he was hoping Angus was willing to play another round.

As I stood up, I caught the far-away look in my father's eyes. It was as if he was seeing something across a great distance. Something I couldn't see. "Angus, is everything okay?"

He didn't answer me. Instead he took two steps back and then his eyes flared wide. "No," he gasped, horror on his face. Then he disappeared, falling backward into a portal that snapped open and closed so fast I had no time to react.

Moose and I stood there, rooted to the spot where the only evidence remaining of my father's presence was the quickly fading scent of brimstone and a small cyclone of sticks and snow that swirled in the air. Everything settled gradually into place again as the wind stirred up by my father's departure faded.

Worry seized me and I took off running back to the house, Moose loping along behind me. The wards would have to wait. Something was wrong and I needed to know what it was.

Chapter Twenty-One

I BURST THROUGH the back door, stumbling into the kitchen. Moose bounded in behind me and slid to a stop, his nails grating as he fought for traction on the floor.

The kitchen was empty. "Cal," I called, catching my breath. I still hated running, but my new training regimen had forced me to develop some endurance, whether I'd wanted to or not. "Cal! Torren!"

The sound of movement came from two areas of the house. The sound of footsteps pounding up the stairs from the basement and down from the second floor reassured me that I'd been heard. Callum was the first into the kitchen, knocking open the basement door, a fierce look on his face. Torren was a second behind, coming into the kitchen from the direction of the living room, clearing the corners of the room with his gun as he entered.

Cal's eyes darted over me, as if he was checking for

injuries. I waved his concern for me away. "I'm fine, but, something's wrong. Angus was here, we were talking about things—and then he was gone." I wrapped my arms around my middle, fear beginning to worm through my gut. "Cal, he was scared."

Understanding dawned on Cal's face and he shot a glance over my head to Torren. "We need to go. Grab a bag."

Torren nodded and left the room without a word. "Laney, did Angus say anything at all before he left? Anything to give you an idea where he was going?"

I shook my head. "We were talking and then it was like he was looking somewhere else. I heard him say the word 'NO' and then he disappeared."

Torren appeared back in the kitchen, a black backpack slung over his shoulder. He handed another one to Callum then looked at me. At my questioning look, he said, "Go bags. Supplies we might want to have." His eyes flicked over me, from head to toe. "Are you armed right now?"

I nodded, my hand sliding around to the holster I wore. It had become a requirement. Another change for me to get used to. I didn't leave the house without at least one weapon on me. "Gun, extra mags. Knife in my boot."

"Then let's go. We've got ourselves a devil to find."

⚡

WE FOLLOWED CAL out to the back yard. As I stepped up beside him, he looked down at me. "I can key a portal to

Angus." At my questioning look, he shrugged. "Let's call it a side effect of our . . . friendship."

"Well, that's good then. You should be able to take us right to him."

He nodded. "I'm kind of wondering if that's what we should do."

"What do you mean? Of course it's what we should do."

Cal turned to face me, his eyes serious. "Delaney, think about it. He left you here, and based on what you told me, it sounds like it was because something scared him badly."

"Exactly."

"So, you tell me, what could possibly scare the Devil himself?"

His question stunned me. He was right, if I thought about it. I'd never seen my father frightened before. Angry, frustrated, conniving, but never afraid. The idea that whatever he'd left to confront could be bad enough to put the amount of fear I'd seen on his face left me shaken.

I grabbed Cal's hand. "I understand what you're saying, but honestly, it doesn't matter. He needs us, Cal. I know he does. I have to be there for him. For whatever this is."

His eyes searched mine. I didn't flinch away from his scrutiny. I let him see it all. My need, my determination.

He finally squeezed my hand. "Okay then. But be ready for whatever we find."

I nodded and let him go. He closed his eyes and took a deep breath, as if steadying himself. He went motionless as

Moose stepped up next to him. I held my breath and waited.

Silence stretched out around us until Callum raised his hands and the portal opened. Wind raced by me, strands of my hair twisting as the vortex spun. Cal glanced back at me and Torren, as if to assure himself we still wanted to do this. I tipped my chin up and met his eyes, not backing down. He gave me a nod and said, "Let's go."

We stepped forward as a team onto the bridge of the portal and were swept away.

Chapter Twenty-Two

THE SCENE I stumbled onto as the portal shut behind me was filled with flames and the taste of ashes on the air. Shock made me gasp as I fought to find my balance on solid ground. Heavy smoke filled my lungs, an acute ache I forced myself to cough out. My eyes watered in reaction to the stinging smoke and I used the hem of my shirt to wipe them clean. When my vision cleared, I took a good look at the scene, trying to understand exactly where we were and what was happening.

My father stood, his back to me, his hands spread out before him as if he would pull the flames into himself.

"Laney," said a low voice, surprising me with its closeness. I turned to my right, Cal's figure flickering as the light from the fire danced and skipped over him. "Stay back. Until we know wha—"

A scream broke through his words and I covered my ears

in reflex. In front of me, I saw Angus sink down to the ground, next to a strange trough in the dirt that ran around the barn burning before us, his body shaking with sobs.

Recognition lit through me. Cal's portal had brought us to my mother's home, the ranch where she'd raised me. And the barn that was burning was her barn. Where our horses lived.

Another scream rose from my father, and this time I heard the word it formed, the heartbreak at its very core. "ANGIE!"

I scrambled forward, fear turning my stomach as I realized what was happening. Cal's hand wrapped around my arm, pulling me back.

"Cal, my mother. She must be inside. We have to get to her." I could hear my father's cries, rising up over the snapping fire. I wrenched myself free and ran to where Angus had collapsed. I fell to my knees beside him, damp earth soaking through the denim I wore. Grabbing his hand, I pulled hard to turn his attention my way. "Dad, we have to get in there. We have to help her."

The green of my father's eyes was almost gone, swallowed up by flames that matched those raging before us. He shook his head, as if trying to clear his mind, and I saw something I'd never seen before on his face. Defeat.

"I can't. I can't get to her. It's keeping me out." He tore his hand free of my grip, reaching forward toward the fire and then reeling back with a hiss of pain as if he'd been struck. It couldn't be the flames. Fire was the Devil's element. Fighting my own fear, I stretched my hand out toward the flames that writhed, consuming more and more of the structure before me. I waited for the sensation to hit me, for the searing pain to begin as my skin reacted to the heat but nothing happened. I had never been impervious to fire, my humanity always rendering me vulnerable. But instead of burning me, the fire leaned toward me, warmth radiating but never burning me.

An idea flashed through me. I called a portal into the space directly in front of me and the air that rushed past as it opened fanned the flames even higher. I didn't wait, knowing someone would try to stop me. Instead, I dove forward, tucking my head and rolling down the semi solid incline of the portal. I heard a voice cry out behind me as the portal snapped shut and I was dumped onto the floor of the barn I'd once known so well.

I sucked in air on reflex and then coughed, the acrid smoke difficult to breathe. The heavy haze made it hard to see, so I dropped to the ground and crawled my way forward. The fire was loud in my ears, raging and snapping as if it was alive, but still, it didn't burn me. I didn't waste time trying to unravel that mystery. I needed to find my mother.

My progress was slow as I checked every possible place that offered shelter from the fire. It was in the corner of the last stall that I found her. My mother was curled up in a ball, unmoving, a jacket of my father's clutched to her middle. I couldn't tell if she was breathing or not.

The overwhelming urge to sob tightened my throat but I fought against it, clinging to hope. I tried to call a portal again, envisioning the smooth ground outside, but I couldn't focus enough to open the path out. The heat was building around us, and fear began to crawl through me. If I didn't find a way out soon, my mom and I might not survive this. I forced myself to process my options calmly, to think of some way out.

One of my recent sparring sessions with Cal clawed its way to the front of my mind. I'd used a controlled burst of energy to fling him away from me. I could do the same with the doors.

I hooked my arms around my mother's waist, and leaned back, pulling the weight of her toward the front of the barn. I sipped at the air, pain flaring in my chest with each tiny breath. I kept my thoughts quiet, focusing on each step that took us closer to the doors.

"Come on, Mom. Only a little bit farther." I refused to think of her as dead weight, even though my arms ached while I dragged her with me.

At the doors, the flames rose up hungrily, hissing as they surged up over the old wood. I closed my eyes and with every ounce of strength I had, I pulled the power I carried into my core and let it fill me up until the hairs on my arm rose and the pressure within me increased to the point I knew I couldn't hold anymore. I opened my eyes and focused on the heavy doors in front of me. Then, with a deep exhale, I let the power go.

My control vanished and the heady power rushed out of me, crashing into the wood, splintering it. The doors fell open and cooler air drifted in as I stumbled forward, pulling my mother out into the night with me.

"Laney!" I heard my name and looked up as Tor and Cal came running to me. Cal pulled my mother from me and lifted her into his arms. Torren wrapped an arm around my waist and supported me as we made our way to where my father and Uncle Newt were standing. I coughed and wished for water to wash away the taste of cinders in my mouth.

As we made our way clear, Angus reached toward Cal, his hand hesitating above my mother's limp arm. Cal ignored him, laying my mother down on the ground and checking her vitals. The flicker of sadness that crossed his face was telling and I felt my knees give way beneath me.

"Cal, please. You have to help her." I pleaded with him, not caring if I looked weak in this moment. I would have bargained away all I had if it meant he would save my mother.

He shook his head as he lifted his eyes to meet mine. "I can't, Delaney. There's nothing I can do. She's gone."

There was a roar above me, grief and pain and loss tangled together in the sound. My father collapsed onto the ground, tears shining in eyes that were no longer the bright green I'd known all my life. Instead, they glowed, flames flickering in the depths and I felt something, deep down in the darkest part of me, sliding forward, out of my control and toward the fire burning in my father's eyes.

A whine in my ear broke the trance I was in as Moose leaned his warm, heavy weight into my side. He licked my cheek and that comforting gesture broke through the restraint I'd held onto so tightly up until this moment. Tears filled my eyes and I didn't fight them as they spilled out.

My father's fingers settled around my arm, twining tightly and crushing down hard, drawing a gasp of pain from me.

"Why were you able to go in there? When I wasn't?" Angus spit the words at me, fury underlying each one. His grip tightened even further as he pulled me forward over my mother's body. Moose's growl sounded behind me, but I couldn't look away from my father's face. Pain was etched into his skin, deep and unmistakable.

"Answer me. Why, Delaney?"

I shook my head. Fear was crawling through me, chasing away the pain and grief, replacing it with a deep desire to get away. To run and put as much distance as possible between myself and my father. Something I'd never experienced before.

"ANSWER ME!" His rage was a power within itself, the impact of it battering at me, and any defenses I might've had in place failed in the face of it. There was a war brewing within him. I watched as the pain on his face was replaced with anger and fury. A crack appeared in his skin, directly above his left eye, a small fissure opening in the rock that had been my father. Red light flashed from it and panic began to take me over.

"I don't know." He dragged me across my mother's body as he stood, and agony flared down my left arm, the scars I'd earned when I was attacked by the Proles demon throbbing. I kept repeating the only answer I had to his question. "I don't know. Dad, I swear, please, I don't know. Please, please, stop."

Moose's growl rumbled, loud and heavy now, and I heard Torren shout, but my focus had narrowed to the man in front of me. The man who I suddenly understood blamed me for the death of my mother. I dug my heels in as he pulled me along, trying to resist, but it was useless. The cracks in him were spreading, lines racing across his skin until red light streamed from him. The flames were dying away around us and he glowed in the near darkness. He was breaking apart and there was nothing I could do.

There was a shout and arms wrapped around my waist, slowing my progress. Angus turned, snarling. He was no longer the man I had always known. Instead, fangs descended from black lips and the planes of his face shifted, his famous curls transforming into horns as I watched, horrified. Glimmering scales slipped into place over his cheekbones and jaw, spilling down onto his throat like interlocking armored plates. There was a tearing sound and leathery wings snapped open behind him. In that moment, the man that had been my father was gone. Instead, the Devil stood before me. He dropped my arm and screamed, the agonized sound ripping through the air around me.

I fell to my knees, covering my ears, and cowered at the feet of the Devil. A breeze lifted the sweaty strands of hair from where they clung to my neck, but I didn't look back. He raised his arm and I waited for the blow, never even thinking to defend myself. This is where we would all end. There was nothing I could do to stop this. Nothing I wanted to do.

Cal appeared between us, driving his fist into the chest of the beast that had once been my father and sending him stumbling back. "My debt is paid," he said, his voice carrying as a raging wind surrounded us. "It is done." Then he turned to me, pulled me to my feet and crushed my lips with his. As he pulled away, he whispered, "I am yours now," and I felt something shift in me, an electric jolt so strong I couldn't move as it raced through me.

"Take her," he said. I felt arms settle around me, my body recognizing Torren before my brain could. He pulled me backwards two steps and then we were falling. I could see Callum, tears on his face, as he turned away from me to face the Devil. Cal opened his hand and called his flaming sword to life, Moose aligned with him, ready to fight. Then the portal snapped shut and they were all lost to me.

We hit hot sand with a painful thump, rolling with our momentum, arms and legs tangling together until we came to a rough stop, Torren's weight heavy on me. A high sun sat above us as we untwined ourselves. Looking around, I couldn't see anything familiar. There was nothing but an endless sea of sand, waves carved out by the wind. I had no idea where we were.

I struggled to my feet, the ground slipping beneath me as I fought for balance and then offered Torren a hand. He gained his feet and swiped at the grains clinging to him as he surveyed our location. He said exactly what I feared.

"Where the hell are we?"

I shook my head and walked a few steps away, shading my eyes. The heat was intense, and I worried that Torren wouldn't last long if we didn't find some shelter and water. Soon.

The rays of the sun glinted off my arm, red light flaring from the gems in the bracelet I still wore. Twisting around, I saw Torren wore his as well. I held my arm up, trying to offer some reassurance, hoping I sounded more confident than I felt. "Cal and Moose should be able to find us with these."

Tor nodded, then eyes widening, pointed behind me. I heard a small pop and spun, the sand shifting beneath my feet throwing off my balance. A rift hung in the air, a bloody glow marking the ragged edges as it grew. I fell back as something stepped out of it right where I'd been standing.

This creature was one I'd never seen before. Mottled yellow skin covered it and black ridges marched up its spine. Golden eyes, feral and predatory, dominated the space above two angled slits I assumed were small nostrils. It snarled, flashing rows of sharp, filthy fangs, before it snapped its mouth shut and came toward me.

I scrambled back, crab walking away from it. The rift behind it widened a fraction as another one, identical to the first, came through, followed by three more. It was now five against two. And I was still stuck on my butt in the sand.

"What in all the Hells?" I wondered. A gunshot ripped through the air, the meaty sound as the bullet made contact distinct in the stillness around us. The creature that had been its target shrieked but kept advancing, even as black viscous fluid leaked out around the wound.

Torren stepped up beside me, his weapon held out before him in a firm grip as he offered me his free hand. I took it, climbing to my feet, and we backed up together, Tor firing as we went. The creatures kept advancing, shaking off the shock of the impacts, their shrill cries cutting through the air with each wound. Tor's grip on my hand tightened, drawing my attention to his face. The look he gave me was grim and I understood. We had limited ammunition and no cover. We needed to fight or flee.

A portal had brought us here. I should be able to get us out of here the same way. "Hold them, Tor." I released his hand and slid behind him, reaching for the magic within me to open our escape. Only to find it wasn't there. I stretched my senses wide, searching for the core of power I'd grown used to living with but there was no response. Panic rose, tightening my throat as it threatened to swamp me, but I forced it back. We needed a solution.

The gun holstered in the small of my back was of little comfort. That was a last resort. We had to find a way out, fast. The sound of bullets hitting flesh was loud behind me but not as loud as the click of the gun when it was empty.

"Delaney, what's going on? We getting out of here or what?" Torren's voice was tight, the strain evident in the way he emphasized the words.

"I'm working on it. Something's wrong." I pulled my Witness from its holster and handed it to him. "Use this while I figure things out." I slapped the spare mags in the palm of his hand and turned away to focus on the problem at hand.

Some of the creatures were down now, their black blood staining the sand around them. The rift they had come through had spread, more creatures spilling out. There were too many and they were starting to circle around us. The fact that we were their intended prey was evident as they never looked away, working as a group to contain us. One of them stepped out of their formation and swiped at Torren. He dodged and shot me a look, worry in his eyes. He kicked out at the creature, hitting it in the leg. It dropped to the sand and snarled.

I closed my eyes, reaching out once again for magic and

caught a sense of raw power, flowing through the ground beneath us. The vein was there, thin but sufficient. It was buried deep. I needed a way to access it.

I heard the bark of the gun and risked a glance behind me as a scream split the air. Torren's shot had found its target, much like his others, but this time the wound appeared to be mortal. The thing's knees buckled, and it dropped awkwardly onto the sand. Its companions lifted their muzzles and drank in the air, their eyes widening in what I took to be shock.

Torren looked at me, surprise written on his face. I answered his unspoken question. "Blessed bullets. Use them wisely." He nodded and turned back to face what remained of the horde. I focused my attention again on the power I'd found. I knelt on the burning sand and took a deep breath before reaching out again. I caught the thread of power and stretched for it, my hands out as if I could grab it. The grains shifted beneath me and I followed the way they flowed, driving my fingers down until they hit solid ground. My palms flat against the bedrock, I tried again to pull the magic up into me. I could sense it, floating on the other side of the barrier. The gems on my bracelet flared again in the bright sunlight, sparking an idea.

I yanked the bracelet off, throwing it onto the hard ground in front of me and pulling my knife from my boot. I flipped it in my hand, grasping the handle tight and slammed the butt cap down onto the leather backing the crystals were affixed to. I heard the gems grinding against the solid surface, but they didn't break. I did it again, driving it down over and over. I knew I was almost there. The pressure building inside me grew. Distantly, I heard Torren yell and the firing of my gun, but it was all muffled. A pounding ache began in my head and I fought against the heavy weight of despair growing in my chest. What I needed felt just out of reach. I stretched myself a shade farther and there it was, the line of power I'd sensed. It was a thin stream of energy, but powerful enough if I could get to it. I summoned all my remaining strength and brought the knife down one more time. The gems gave way beneath the force and exploded, releasing the power stored in them straight down and breaking through the barrier between me and the magic. I opened myself to it, let it fill me and then bundled it into one usable jolt of energy. Enough to power a doorway to somewhere safe.

I channeled the energy from its source through my body. The hairs on my arms stood up as the air around me became suddenly charged. Torren shouted again but I didn't look back this time. "Open," I whispered to myself, my lips barely moving. The light in front of me changed, shifting until a small portal appeared, our way out of here. I stepped toward it, my hand outstretched, but the firing of my gun pulled my attention away from what was in front of me.

"Torren, we have to go." I glanced back to where he stood, still facing down the monsters. The energy of the portal was sporadic and unstable, rising and falling in a way I was having trouble controlling.

"*Leave him.*" The words in my head were dark, the voice unrecognizable. "*Leave him and go. You're the only one who matters.*"

I nodded and took a step to the portal, then forced myself to stop. I couldn't leave Torren behind. The voice came again. "*He's nothing. Leave him.*" My feet began to move, outside my control, and fear rose up. This was new. Terrifying.

"I can't. I have to help him." I said the words out loud, repeating them over and over, a mantra to myself. Desperate, I yelled to him. "Torren, please. We have to leave now. I can't hold it here much longer."

He shot once more and then spun, running toward me. My feet had found their way onto the shining edge of the bridge and I fought against the desire to move faster. I refused to escape without him. Already I could see the edge of the portal beginning to fray, the silver bridge in the air shrinking.

Tor had almost reached me when one of the creatures got a claw around his ankle. Torren went down, slipping on the shifting sands and another one grabbed his arm. Something within me reared up, satisfaction and anticipation spiking. It felt like darkness was weaving its way through my core, changing me. For a moment, I was paralyzed but then Torren cried out, a frantic sound. "Delaney, help!"

I shook off the paralysis and launched myself toward him. As my feet hit the sand once again, I felt the earth tip, the power I'd been holding so tightly shifting with my change in position. The sparks within the portal flared and it began to shrink even faster. I grabbed Torren's hand and lurched back, dragging him away from the grasping creatures. He struggled to get his feet under him and in a few steps, we were moving. In his free hand, he held my gun, and he looked back once, firing a shot that was followed immediately by a pain-filled scream. The portal was failing, even as I focused my attention on it again. Torren's weight was heavy, but I forced us on, determination fueling me. I held my connection with the magic tightly, refusing to let any more of it slip away and the portal stabilized a fraction. We stumbled onto the shining path and I gasped in relief. My guard dropped, and right when I thought we were safe, Torren was pulled backward. It was only my arm around his waist that kept him from being torn completely away from me. The portal flickered, the magic faltering as my concentration was interrupted and I grabbed him tighter. I wrapped my other arm around him, pulling him to me in an awkward hug, and fell backward. I saw the mouth of the creature that had grabbed at him over his shoulder, fangs arching down and burying themselves in the meat of him. I closed my eyes and pushed the magic away, releasing it. The portal snapped shut, taking us to the safest place I could imagine.

Chapter Twenty-Three

WE LANDED ON a hard surface, Torren's weight heavy on top of me. He groaned in pain as I rolled him off to the side. Blood covered his back and my hands. I blanched at the sight of the creature's head and half of its torso, the teeth still buried in Tor's shoulder. When the portal closed, it had cut the beast in half. I didn't feel the least bit bad about that.

"We made it?" The question was soft, the words hesitant.

"We did. For now." I tried to sound reassuring. "But we need to get you cleaned up. Lay still while I find some supplies."

I scrambled out from under his legs, the grit of the sand that covered us both making me itch for a shower. I kept my eyes averted from the remains of the creature, a concern that would have to be dealt with soon enough. I found my way to the master bathroom in Callum's apartment, pulling towels and washcloths from the linen closet. Gauze, medical tape and a bottle of rubbing alcohol were under the sink. Standing up, I risked a glance in the mirror. Ash streaked my face. Cuts and bruises I didn't remember earning were clearly visible. But the thing that frightened me the most were my eyes. The green was still there, but something about them had changed. I leaned in, searching for what was different and couldn't pin it down, but the certainty wouldn't leave me. There was a darkness in them now, a shadow. Terror swelled up, catching in my throat and making me want to vomit. I forced it down, giving myself a few spare moments before I had to face Torren.

I ran some hot water, scrubbing at my hands with soap so they'd at least be clean as I tended his wound and got him stabilized. I'd deal with the rest of the mess later. I dried my hands, my worries wandering to Callum and Moose. Hoping they were okay and that they would find us soon, somehow. With the loss of my bracelet, they wouldn't be able to use it to track me. But they should be able to follow the one Torren wore.

As I walked back into the room with supplies in hand, Tor looked at me from his position against the wall. Based on the trail of blood, he'd managed to dislodge the creature's teeth from his shoulder then crawled to the corner where he could use the structure to brace himself. His head rested against the hard surface and my gun was on the floor beside him. His gaze flicked between me and the remains of the creature that had tried to follow us through the portal.

"You all right?" he asked, pain coating every word.

I nodded. "I'm fine. You're the one we need to worry about right now."

He shrugged then gasped in pain, his body curving inward. The movement caused the fabric of his shoulder to gape open above his injury and I winced at the thought of how much more cleaning his wound was going to hurt him.

"I hate to do this, but you know I've got to look at that bite and clean it up. Can't have it getting infected. I'd have to carry the load all the time then." I winked at him when his eyes focused on my face and he gave me a half-hearted quirk of the lips in response.

He shifted slightly, carefully turning so he was still supported by the wall with his shoulder accessible. I set everything down as I knelt beside him on the cool floor. I grabbed the edges of fabric that were already torn and pulled. The material came apart easily in my hands. I grabbed a cloth and began to wipe away the blood covering his wound. As the skin came clean, I sucked in a breath at the depth of the bite. The area around it was bruising already, and I scanned Tor's face anxiously. His jaw was tight, clenched in pain.

"Can I get you something right now? Before I sterilize this?"

He shook his head, gritting his teeth even more with that simple movement. I took a deep breath and gave his hand a quick squeeze before grabbing the bottle of rubbing alcohol I'd found. When I eased the cap off, the distinctive sharp smell hit me full in the face. It reminded me of skinned knees after my mom taught me how to ride my bike. It was an odor that was oddly comforting even while my muscles clenched in anticipation of the discomfort to come. I slowly poured the alcohol over the gash, holding one of the washcloths close to his skin to catch the runoff. Torren flinched as the liquid flowed down, then held himself rigid as I continued my work. I forced myself to focus on what I was doing, pushing the steady ache I could feel in him through our bond to the back of my mind. I could've blocked it out, shut down our connection, but that seemed unfair. He'd gotten hurt protecting me. I couldn't cut him off. That would only wound him further.

I talked as I worked, hoping to distract Tor and myself from the pain of the process. "Moose and Cal will find us. They should be able to track your bracelet even though mine's gone."

"Mine is too. Torn off by those damn things back there."

"Oh." I tried not to let my worry at his admission show. "Well, I'm sure it'll be all right. They'll find us somehow."

When I was satisfied that it was clean and no longer bleeding, I pressed the gauze into place, securing it with the medical tape. I offered Torren a hand up, but he waved me away.

"I'll stay right here. Have to keep an eye on what's left of our new friend over there." I followed his attention over to the body of the monster that had almost made it here with us.

"I'm pretty sure he's done. That portal chopped him in half like it was nothing when it snapped shut."

Torren snorted at that. "It should've known better. After all, three's a crowd," he said, wincing as he laughed at his own joke.

I grinned as I walked away, heading to the kitchen. We needed time for Torren to rest and while we waited, it would be smart to rehydrate. The desert had been hot and dry. Even I was feeling the effect. Eating something would be a good idea too. Tor was too weak for me to risk draining him of energy because I wasn't fueling myself.

Cal's pantry still had some protein bars lined up on the shelves, organized alphabetically by flavor. I thought back to the condition of my kitchen before he'd arrived, the haphazard way I'd put things away. All that had changed once Cal settled in. I gave a wicked little laugh under my breath and flicked a finger out, scattering the bars from their ordered arrangement before grabbing a few and sticking them in my pockets. I could easily imagine the look on Cal's face when he found what I'd done, the frown and then the grin he'd give me. Giving in to the burst of temptation, I moved on to his other cabinets, swapping things around, mixing glasses with plates, bowls mismatched with mugs. I indulged myself for a few minutes, then filled two cups with water straight from the tap and carried them out to where Torren was resting. His eyes were closed, but there was still a watchfulness about him. I set the water near his hand, where it would be easy for him to reach on his uninjured side. I picked up the gun and was in the process of sliding it back into its holster when Torren's touch on my arm stopped me. His eyes were open and focused intently on me. Even though I'd purposely limited our one-on-one interactions, trying to keep physical contact at a minimum to help him manage the overwhelming progression of the bond, I didn't pull away from him this time.

"Thank you." The words were low and raw, like his throat hurt and he licked his lips as if they were too dry to say much more. "For getting us out of there."

I didn't say anything in response to that, only giving him a nod in acknowledgment. Then I handed him the cup of water. "Drink this. That place sucked you dry. It's going to be hard for you to heal if you're dehydrated. We've got to take advantage of resources while we can right now."

He took the water from me and drank deep until it was emptied. I traded him the empty cup for one of the protein bars and headed back to the kitchen to fill it up again. When I returned, he dutifully drank half of it before setting it aside. I joined him on the floor, leaning back against the wall and letting my eyes close for a moment.

His voice brought me right back to reality. "You brought us to Cal's place, didn't you?"

"Yeah. It was the first place I could think of that would be safe for us."

Tor paused, a hesitation that hinted of hurt. "It looks

like him."

I chuckled at that. "I had the same thought. It suits him."

"You've been here before?"

"Once. To help him get some stuff after Angus assigned him to stay with me."

"And you thought this would be the safest place for us after everything that's happened?"

I was surprised by the question. In truth, I hadn't thought it through quite that specifically. When I'd opened the portal, my thought had been on escaping where we were as quickly as possible. Safe had been my only focus. I supposed that was a sign Cal's home and safety were linked in my mind.

"Honestly, I haven't opened a portal to very many other places before. This seemed like a good idea in the moment."

Tor sighed. "Do you trust him?"

"Cal?" I asked, unsure of why he would ask me that. "Of course I do. He's saved us both more than once. He even got us out of there tonight."

"He sent us to a desert where creatures were waiting to kill us." The comment was low, hard to hear. But there was a certainty in the tone I didn't miss.

"You're assuming he knew they'd be there. We don't know where they came from, or even what they were exactly. Anyone could be responsible for those things." His distrust of Callum was nothing new. It had grown stronger over time, more evidence of how the bond was poisoning him. Changing him.

"I'm looking at the way things line up. He's always there when something goes wrong, to step in and save you at the last second. He comes out looking like a hero." He paused, taking another drink of water. "And he never leaves you alone if I'm around. Makes me wonder what he has to be worried about."

I didn't want to tell him that Cal's constant presence was at my request. I could sense how the bond was affecting Torren. His actions had become more erratic, and I'd been worried that time spent alone with me would increase the downward spiral. But I couldn't let him believe that Cal was something that he wasn't.

I took a deep breath. "Cal was only doing what I asked him to do."

Torren froze beside me, in the process of opening one of the protein bars I handed him. "What are you talking about?"

"I asked him to run interference to keep some distance between us."

"You asked him to chaperone us?" There was something like shock in the way he asked the question, as if this had never occurred to him.

"I guess." I shrugged, uncomfortable and grateful I didn't have to look at him while we discussed this issue. "You've been acting differently. Ever since you were gone for a couple days and then came back, you aren't the same. Cal and I were both worried that the bond has been doing something to you. That it's even stronger now than it was before. I thought that maybe if we were always in a group, the bond would ease up a little. That it would make things better for you."

I felt the vibration run through me as his head fell back against the wall. I snuck a glance at his face, stricken by the look of hurt and defeat I saw there. "I'm sorry, Tor. I was trying to help you."

When he finally spoke again, his words were soft and haunted. "Why didn't you tell me, about the bond getting worse?"

"I didn't know how." That felt inadequate, even if the statement was true. "I kept hoping that if we could limit how much time we were together, we'd have a better chance of finding a way to break the connection."

"Any progress on that?"

This time it was my head that fell back against the wall. "No. Uncle Newt's been working on it, but he hasn't found anything new that will work. Not really."

"What does *not really* actually mean?"

"It means he hasn't found anything I'm willing to risk trying."

"Do I get a say in this at all?"

I closed my eyes. "If it involves a high probability of you dying or going insane, I'm not okay with it. You have to trust me on this."

"I'm already going crazy, the way things are now."

I didn't say anything, allowing the silence to stretch around us. As much as I wanted to find a way to break the connection between us, I couldn't risk losing him. I wanted to set him free. Not ruin his life.

"I shouldn't have kissed you."

His quiet words surprised me. The pain that resonated through me was a shock as well. I hadn't realized he'd regretted that moment, but I couldn't blame him. The truth still hurt.

"Nothing to be done about it now, Tor. Rest while we wait and please, believe me. I'm going to keep looking for an answer to fix this."

"I know you will."

Not knowing what to say, I didn't offer a response. Within a few minutes, Tor's breathing evened out, telling me he was finally sleeping. I took the opportunity to get to my feet and stretch muscles that had gone stiff from abuse and lack of movement. My stomach growled as I cleaned up the mess I'd made treating Torren's wounds, so I forced myself to nibble one of the protein bars.

I turned on the television, keeping the sound down low but needing some distraction. Cal hadn't canceled the utilities, for which I was grateful. Flipping through the channels, I stopped only when a familiar scene caught my eye. It was a photograph of my mother's ranch, the place I'd grown up. It had been taken shortly after the plane crash that had killed Angus Murphy and everyone on it. The staged crash. In it, my mother had her arm around me, pressed close to her side. We'd addressed the crowd that had gathered outside the property together. It was the last time she'd ever asked me to do anything like that. I closed my eyes, remembering the feel of her, small but strong, as she held me up when grief had taken hold back then. She'd endured too much. It felt like I'd failed her in so many ways.

The voices droned on, reporting that a fire on the property had been confirmed. Arson was suspected. First responders were on scene and a body had been found. One that they had identified as Angelique Helena Murphy. My throat tightened as grief swelled up within me. I'd already known she was dead but hearing it like this made it feel too real. As the news anchor promised updates, a video appeared on the screen.

"In remembrance of Mrs. Murphy, the wife of Angus Murphy, we play the last song recorded by Angus Murphy and The Law, before they were also taken too soon—Judas Kiss."

The chords that sounded as the video began rang through me. I closed my eyes, not needing to see the scenes play out. I knew them by heart. I sang softly along with the verse, as I remembered.

Midnight in the garden, I handed you my heart
No hint of the cost, how it would tear us apart
The gift of forever, a promise I could keep
Not knowing the path, the souls it would reap

The music swelled, a crash of drums carrying me into

the chorus, and tears ran down my face. I didn't bother to wipe them away.

Love will betray you, like a Judas Kiss
Love will betray you, like a Judas Kiss
My love betrayed you, like a Judas Kiss

Sitting there in front of the television, the music soaking into every part of me, I didn't move until the song finished, and the reporter was back. My name was mentioned but I couldn't listen to any more and turned it off. Torren's slight snoring told me he was still asleep, and my breakdown hadn't disturbed him. Resolute, I wiped the tears from my cheeks and stood. I needed something to do.

I wandered through Cal's apartment, fingers trailing over the books he'd left on the shelves when he came to stay with me. Tucked into a corner was a framed photograph of Cal and a striking young woman, caught in a happy moment. I picked it up and held it close, examining their posture and closeness. I could almost hear the laughter spilling out of them. I couldn't stop myself from wondering who she was.

I heard a sound, a shuffling really, outside the front door of the apartment. I spun, the picture falling from my grip and landing with a crack at my feet. I raced to the kitchen, sliding a large chef's knife from the block on the counter and testing its balance. I slipped a second one into the top of my boot, the hidden sheath an advantage I was thankful for in this moment. I'd lost my knife in the damn desert. These would work fine as replacements for the time being. Then I took up a position between Torren and the approaching threat.

The lock clicked over and I held my breath as the door swung open. A small sleek shape bounded through the opening toward me, nails scratching across the floor. I'd never been so happy to see a Hell Hound before in my life, even one disguised as a ridiculously large Yorkie.

I scratched behind Moose's ears as he pressed against me. I wasn't surprised to see Cal follow my Hound into the apartment. I offered him a relieved smile.

"I knew you'd find us."

He gave me a short nod, exhaustion evident in the set of his shoulders and the way he dropped down onto the couch after he closed and locked the door. He discarded the two black backpacks he'd carried in with him.

"Are you okay?" I asked. Worry that he'd been wounded or that something else had happened began to well up from my core.

He shifted, turning his head to look directly at me. "Delaney, we need to talk."

Chapter Twenty-Four

I HATED THOSE words. Something bad was coming, even worse than what had already happened. I joined him on the couch, resisting the urge to lean toward him.

"Before you say anything else, please, are you all right?" I heard the hesitancy in my voice, the fear lacing my words, but I didn't try to hide it. I needed to know that he wasn't hurt. Leaving Cal and Moose behind was something I was struggling to forgive myself for, even if I hadn't been given a choice in the moment.

The smile he gave me was small and tired, but it was still a smile. "I'm okay. Sore, a little bloody, but nothing that won't heal with a little rest."

The breath I'd been holding as I waited for his answer rushed out and relief swelled within me. "Hells, you and Moose had me worried, Cal."

"I know," he said, swiping his hand over his face, smearing

the dirt and ash that coated his skin. "But we have to talk about what happened back there."

"My dad," I said, stopping myself and taking a deep breath before I continued. "Is he...?" Fear bloomed in my throat, choking the rest of my words.

The look Cal gave me was sad. "Angus is," he swallowed, looking down at the floor as he leaned forward, propping his elbows on his knees and dropping his head into his hands. "Angus is gone."

Cold flashed through me as I processed what he'd said, not wanting it to be true. "Gone? How can he be gone?" Tears welled and spilled out of my eyes, and I wrapped my arms tight around my middle, trying to stave off the shivers I could feel building. Reality was crashing down around me. In one night, one sudden painful moment, I'd lost both my parents. I was alone.

A flash of warmth spread through me and I looked up in surprise. Cal's hand was resting on my knee and I could feel waves of comfort radiating from him. "What are you doing?" I gasped the question.

"You're hurting. I can feel it." He moved his hand from my leg to his chest. "I can feel it in here. I only want to help you."

"How?" I asked. When he didn't answer, the realization speared through me as the warmth from his touch faded and I ached for it to return. "A Bond. Oh no. You bound yourself to me back there."

"Seemed like a good idea at the time." He shrugged and

gave me a grin. "I had to get you out of there, and I couldn't let Angus keep me from you. So, here we are."

Another Bond. Another life tied to mine. A sob broke loose in my chest as I tried to find somehow to explain this away. "Can you dissolve it? Reverse it somehow?" I sounded crazy, my words piling on top of each other, but I was scrambling. Then hope rose. If he knew how to create a bond between us, maybe he had learned how to fix the accidental one that had trapped Torren in this life.

"Do you know how to fix the bond between me and Torren?"

His eyes were sad as my words faded away into the quiet of the apartment. Hurt coated his voice when he answered my first question. "Is that really what you want, Delaney? To be free of me?"

Regret swelled in my chest. I hadn't meant to wound him. But the idea of being responsible for him, for his life as well as Torren's, was overwhelming.

When I didn't respond, he looked away from me. "If I knew how to dissolve a bond, I'd have told you months ago. I know how desperately you want to free Torren. I wouldn't have kept that knowledge from you."

"Then why would you create one between us? Without talking to me about it first, giving me some warning?" Rational thought fled, replaced again by the fear that here was someone else depending on me. His life irrevocably linked with mine.

"Well, let's see. Your father was losing himself to grief, you weren't defending yourself, and I wasn't about to let you be killed in that confrontation. I also couldn't risk him calling me back, keeping me from protecting you. The bond was a safeguard for us both in that moment." He sighed, shoulders slumping down. "Don't get me wrong. I'd been thinking about it for a while. Had planned to ask if it was something you would want, with me. But the situation we were in, well, I did what I thought was best. To save you. If you hate me for it, I'm sorry."

"I don't hate you." The words spilled out of me before I had the chance to even really think about it, proof they were completely true. I didn't hate him for this at all. "I'm, well, honestly, I'm shocked. It never occurred to me that a bond was something you'd want to have with me."

He shook his head, a small smile on his lips. "Sometimes you're brilliant, Laney. Other times, you're oblivious."

I tried to smile, but I couldn't meet his eyes. There were so many thoughts swirling in my mind. My heart beat faster as I envisioned that scene outside the burning barn one more time. My father's anger and grief felt almost tangible in the memory, as did his fury and rage. Tears threatened to spill down my cheeks as the loss of him began to feel real.

"Did you kill him?" I was afraid of the answer, but I needed to know. Was I truly alone? "Did you kill Angus?"

Cal's hand covered mine, resting in my lap. "I stopped him. I wounded him. And my debt is paid. As soon as we could get away, Moose and I left. Then we started looking for you and Torren."

"Where did you send us in the portal? I didn't recognize anything there."

"What are you talking about? The portal I called was supposed to take you home."

"Well, it didn't. We landed in a desert." I took a deep breath, throwing a quick look at Torren over my shoulder to make sure he was still sleeping. "There were these creatures that came after us there. Through a rift."

"Creatures?" Cal asked. "What were they?"

"I don't know, but one of them hitched a ride here with us. The portal cut it in half when it closed behind us. Come on, I'll show you."

I stood up and led Cal to where the remains of the creature lay on the floor. I hadn't gotten around to cleaning it up. Cal knelt beside the thing's head, flipping it over and examining its features. He then leaned in and gave it a sniff.

"I've never seen anything like this before," he said. "Tell me about when you were attacked. Did the creatures look different? Or were they all the same?"

I thought back to the battle we'd fought. Closing my eyes, I envisioned the scene again. "They were all the same. Stepping through the rift and coming right for us."

Cal's next question was unexpected. "What did you fight them with?"

"Bullets. Tor was shooting them. He hit them, but they just kept coming. Until we switched to my ammo."

"Blessed bullets?" Cal asked. "You had those with you?"

I nodded. "That's when we actually seemed to wound them." Pieces connected in my mind suddenly. "Wait, you think these things are demons?"

"Well, blessed bullets hurt them, and this one smells like rotten brimstone."

I leaned in, recognizing the scent he was referring to as soon as I got closer to the severed head. But I knew demons, and I'd never seen anything like these before. "Where did they come from? I don't recognize them at all."

Cal frowned. "I don't either, which worries me." He turned his gaze to me. "So, someone hijacked my portal, then sent you and Torren somewhere I wouldn't think to look. And only blessed bullets hurt them. You weren't able to use magic against them?"

I flinched at the question. "I tried, but nothing would come. Even opening the portal to here was difficult. I had to pull magic from deep underground to get it to open, and it didn't feel very stable. It took a lot of energy for me to keep it open long enough to get Tor into it."

Cal's eyes dropped to the floor as I explained how we had escaped. "What do you know, Cal? What's wrong?"

"Your magic. The reason it's not coming to you ... your father has cut you off."

The skin on my arms prickled, cold creeping through

me. "What do you mean he cut me off? How could he cut me off from my magic? It's part of me."

Cal shook his head. "It's part of you because you're part of him, Laney. He carries Hell within him. You chose not to. He's cut you off, blocked you from the source. The only magic you have access to now is residual Earth magic. That's what you used to open the portal to come here. That's why it was so hard to do."

"Well, what about you? And Moose?" The idea of all of us being without our magic was terrifying. I heard the quaver in my voice. Moose came to my side at the sound of his name, his small form pressing up against my leg, a low keening sound escaping him. I dropped a hand to his head, stroking the soft fur there.

"Moose is, well, he's stuck right now."

"What do you mean, stuck?"

"He can't shift form. He's stuck like this until he can access his source again."

I looked down at my dog, his rising whine increasing my distress. "He's cut off too." I petted him, cooing nonsense for a moment to try to calm him before returning my attention to Cal. "And what about you?"

Cal looked away and the uneasy feeling in my stomach began to spread. "I'm . . .," he paused, taking a deep breath before continuing. "I'm complicated."

Chapter Twenty-Five

"What's that supposed to mean?" I asked the question, trying to cover the tension in my voice with humor. "Everyone's complicated. I mean, look at me. And Tor. We're definitely complicated."

As if responding to his name, Torren gave a groan and shook himself from where he rested against the wall. I rose from the couch but then turned back to Cal. We needed to continue this conversation, after we'd checked on Tor's wounds. "Would you help me with him? You can make sure I haven't missed anything when I was cleaning him up."

Cal hesitated, then nodded, joining me as we walked over to where Tor was stirring. I touched Cal's arm, wanting to reassure him, and whispered, "We'll talk. I promise." He gave my hand a gentle squeeze then released me to kneel beside Torren.

I held my breath as Callum checked over my work on

Tor's injuries. He lifted the dressing off, giving the torn edges of skin his clinical evaluation. I worried as I waited that there might be something I had missed.

"Not too bad. You've learned a lot already." Cal looked up at me, giving me a proud grin.

I felt the warmth of a blush spreading across my skin. "Thanks. I had a good teacher."

"Hate to interrupt, but this floor is pretty damn uncomfortable, you know." Torren's sleepy voice broke the connection between me and Cal. "Any chance I can move to the couch? Or maybe even a bed?"

I laughed, appreciating the release of tension. Cal replaced the bandages before Tor was ready to attempt standing. I jumped in to help Tor to his feet and Cal supported him on the other side, then directed us to the master bedroom. Torren leaned heavily on us both, exhaustion and pain evident in the way he moved. He gave a sigh when we reached the bed and lowered him carefully to the mattress. Cal helped him get his shoes off and swing his legs up. I covered him with the comforter. He whispered a soft, "Thank you," before his eyes closed again, and his breathing evened out. I turned the light off and closed the door quietly, wishing Tor rest and healing as I prepared for whatever waited for us next.

Chapter Twenty-Six

MOOSE GREETED ME with a lift of his head from where he rested on the living room couch. I dropped my hand to the soft fur between his ears, stroking over the spot gently and he gave a sigh, licking my fingers once before closing his eyes and laying his head down again. I waited, wanting to hear the words he'd whispered to me before, the ones that reminded me I wasn't alone. *Friend. Family.* His strong, quiet voice in my mind was soothing when he chose to share his thoughts with me. Tonight, there was nothing between us but silence and then his cute little snores as he too fell asleep. I watched him with a small smile on my face before it stretched into a large yawn. Hells, I was tired. I sank down onto the couch, closing my eyes, the events of the day finally sinking in as exhaustion deepened its hold on me.

A soft blanket settled over me and I protested, knowing I needed to tend to things. A part of my mind demanded I wake and seek the answers I needed. Cal's voice shushed me, and I felt the tiredness take root, pulling me down into sleep. I heard the unmistakable command in his words even as he whispered them to me. "Rest now." There was the gentle pressure of his lips as he kissed my forehead, the spice cake scent of him surrounding me. Then he was gone, and my resolve failed. I slept.

DREAMS ARE TRICKY things. This one felt real. So real, that when my mother's face emerged from the fog surrounding me, I fell to my knees and cried out in pain as I hit the rocky ground. Relief sparked inside as I reached out to her. The warmth of her hand as it closed around mine eased the chill that had invaded me since I'd lost her.

Bit by bit, the fog dissipated until my mother was free and fully revealed. There were no burns or wounds, no evidence of pain in her expression. I didn't have the strength to get up from my knees or fight the tears rolling from my eyes.

"Laney. My sweet girl." Her voice was the same as it had always been, sweet and kind, drawing me in and making me trust that she would always be there. To listen. To guide. Her hands stroked my hair then pulled me close. I wrapped my arms around her middle, needing to hold her here. "I'm sorry I couldn't stay with you."

I shook my head, breathing in the comforting scent I'd

always associated with her—citrus and sugar, like the candied oranges she'd given me when I was little. "I need you. Please don't go." I heard the childish hurt in the words as they left me, but I didn't care about my pride. Here, in this space, I could be a girl who was afraid and wanted the solace only her mother could give. No one would ever know that I wasn't always strong. My mother would never share this secret. I could confess anything, and it would forever stay between the two of us. "I'm scared. Without you, I don't know what to do."

My mother's arms tightened around me, hugging me to her. She let me stay there, the comfort of her touch spreading through me, until my tears slowed and the hitch in my breathing was smoothed away.

"Look at me, sweetheart." She tipped my chin up, forcing me to meet her eyes. "This is only the beginning for you. There's so much left to be done and only you can do these things. Find your father again. Return him to himself."

Pain speared my chest at those words, and I tried to push away from her. "He hates me now." Shame crawled through me as I explained my failure. "I wasn't strong enough to save you. He's cut me off." The ache of truth, my real fear, forced me to continue. "He blames me for losing you. He'll never forgive that."

"Laney, there was nothing you could have done. My death was planned. To weaken your father, to hurt you. It was always going to be this way."

Confusion swelled in me. "But why? You've never done anything but try to help people. Who would want to do this to you? To us?"

Sadness filled her eyes as she looked down at me. "There have always been those who were jealous for your father's attention. With his love directed to me, and then you as well, that jealousy poisoned them even further. It was simply a matter of time before they tried to destroy what he loved. I knew that long ago. When you came into your powers, I was so relieved. It was a layer of protection I could never have given you. It gave you a chance to learn about those who would become your enemies."

Shock spiraled through me at the idea that she'd been happy I'd inherited my father's power. Loneliness filled my chest, an ache echoing in my gut. I needed her to stay. "I can't do this alone. Please." I didn't care that I begged. I'd do anything to keep her with me. "If you talk to Dad, we can fix things. We can find a way to bring you back."

A sound rang out, breaking through the heavy mist around us. My mother looked over her shoulder, her eyes on something I couldn't see. She shook her head, then turned back to me. "That is not a choice available to us now. Things are as they must be. Find your father. Remind him of who he truly is. You can do this."

Slowly, as if she hated to let me go, she released me and stepped back. The fog crept in again, blurring the space between us, the edges of her body beginning to fade.

"Please, Mom. I don't know how to solve this. Please, help me." Tears came again, tears I never cried when awake. "Please don't leave me alone."

Her voice was barely audible, as it fought against the mist that shrouded us in its clinging dampness. "You're not alone, Laney. Let your angel guide you."

I kept my eyes on her, needing to drink in the vision of her as long as I could. Her mouth opened one final time, but then there was a shadow behind her, a presence that reared up. Arms wrapped around her, one covering her mouth and the other encircling her waist. Her eyes went wide and then she was gone, pulled back into swirling blackness. Then there was nothing left but silence and she was truly gone, the fog swelling around me until I thought I would choke. I gasped for breath and came awake, the warmth of Moose at my side and the sound of his snores letting me know I was once again in the real world. I shivered, the cold of the dream having followed me and penetrated into my bones. I pulled the blanket tighter and even though I desperately wanted to keep my eyes open, sleep claimed me again. Thankfully, there were no more dreams.

Chapter Twenty-Seven

WHEN I WOKE again, it was morning, a dim light beginning to break through the windows. Cal was already up, moving around in the kitchen. Moose had moved from where he'd been sleeping next to me and was now sitting on the floor next to the couch, his head cocked to the side and a worried look on his sweet face. I couldn't hear anything from him, but I didn't need to in this moment.

"I'm fine. I promise." I reached out and offered him my hand, holding still until he ducked his head down and let me pet his head. "But we've got things to work on. Can't have you stuck like this forever, can we?"

He allowed me one last scratch behind his ears before he trotted off, likely toward whatever food had been set aside for him. It felt like that dog was always eating.

Cal walked into the living room as Moose left it. I grinned at the look they gave each other in passing. I suspected that even though he was trapped in the form of a small dog, Moose had some way of communicating with Cal. Even if it was only because they knew each other so well.

I gratefully accepted the mug Callum extended toward me, appreciating the scent of tea brewing. I sipped at it carefully, setting it down on the coffee table. Cal took a seat in the opposite corner of the couch, angling himself toward me as he drank from a mug of his own.

"Coffee?" I asked, sure of the answer.

He grimaced as he set the mug down. "Instant. But it's all I've got right now. Desperate times, desperate measures. All my good stuff is at your house."

I nodded, remembering his insistent need to have his specialty coffee on hand when he moved into my place. His comment made me think of home. My stomach twisted as I realized how much I longed to be there.

"Do you think it's safe? For us to go back there?" I asked the question quietly, dropping my eyes to the blanket that I was gripping tightly in my fingers. I'd made the old farmhouse my home, caring for the dwelling and the land surrounding it exactly as I'd promised its previous owner I would. The idea that I might lose it as well hurt me more than I'd ever thought it could.

Cal sighed. "Well, we can't stay here for much longer. If Torren's up to it, we should probably get moving today."

"But do you think we can go home?" As I said the words, I realized that I thought of that home as belonging to all of us now. What had once been mine alone had transformed into a place I associated with the four of us.

"I think we need to be careful. Safe. But we can check on it, see what things look like."

I took that as a positive and the feeling motivated me to get up. "Perfect. I'll get cleaned up and you can check on Torren." I snagged my cup from the table, carrying it with me as I headed toward the bathroom.

"Laney," Cal called out. "We still need to have that talk."

I waved at him as I walked away. "We will. We will."

I DIDN'T NEED TO dig around in the cabinets of Cal's bathroom to find what I needed to clean myself up. A fresh toothbrush and a tube of toothpaste waited for me on the vanity top. A washcloth lay on top of a folded towel with an unopened bar of soap. I sighed. The man knew me too well. He'd anticipated that I'd cling to my routine, understanding the comfort it offered me.

I brushed my teeth, then jumped into the shower. The warmth of the spray surrounding me eased muscles I hadn't realized were tense and sore from the battle yesterday. It also washed away the stink that had infused itself into my skin and hair. Cal had been right when he'd referred to it as rotten brimstone. The soap he'd left for me was simple, unscented and exactly what I needed. The small bottle of shampoo I'd found tucked into the corner shelf of the shower was also unscented. I watched the water swirl around my feet, gradually turning from a dirty gray until it finally ran clear. I gave myself permission to relax under the hot water for a little bit longer before I turned it off. There were things that had to be done.

I stepped out and wrapped the heavy towel around me, right as there was a knock at the door. I snugged the towel tight and opened the door a crack, leaning around it to find Cal standing there.

"Here, you can wear these. Found them in one of the backpacks. We tried to plan ahead." He offered a folded pile of clothes to me. "Your clothes from yesterday are a wreck and we don't have a lot of time before we need to leave."

I accepted the clothes awkwardly, one hand clinging to my towel as I reached the other through the gap between the door and the jamb. "Thank you."

He nodded, turning to go. Then he glanced back to me. "Torren's waking up. His shoulder looks much better. You did a good job with it last night."

I smiled as he turned away, pride filling me at hearing those words. Torren had been hurt fighting beside me, but I'd been able to take care of him. It eased the regret I felt a bit.

Pulling on the sweatshirt Cal had brought me, I breathed in the spicy scent of him clinging to the fabric. The pants were an old pair I hadn't worn in a while. They were too big, the constant, focused training with Cal having whittled me down. The waistband gapped a little, but Cal was right, these would do.

Torren was up and moving around unaided when I emerged from the bathroom. The small smile that spread across his face when he spotted me was encouraging. Rest had done him good. The shadows under his eyes had faded and there was less heaviness about him.

"Do we have enough time that I can shower too?" he asked, clearly aware we weren't staying here.

Cal nodded. "Sure. Be careful with your shoulder, though. It's looking better. Don't want to make it worse."

Torren gave me an assessing glance as he passed. "Got any extra clothes for me, Cal? I'd even accept some of your hand-me-downs if I had to." There was the hint of a teasing tone to the words and I slapped his uninjured shoulder gently in response as I passed him. I appreciated the lighter feeling between the three of us here. The constant tension that had been building had affected us all.

Cal's chuckle lifted the mood even more. "You packed the bags. Better hope you chose wisely."

He placed a mug of tea in front of me then grabbed one of the black backpacks from the floor and carried it to where Torren was leaning against the bathroom door. I sipped at my tea, enjoying the calm, comfortable way I was feeling. It had been a long time since I'd felt this way. It reminded me of times I'd spent with my parents, when were all able to be together. A family. Then I was reminded that I'd lost them both, my mother to the fire and my father to his devastation. I was without them for the first time in my life. They weren't there for me to call when I needed help. Or even a listening ear. Loneliness crashed over me, the heaviness of it making it hard to hold my head up.

"Way to ruin the mood there, Laney." I whispered the words before taking another drink. I tried to shake off the sadness that had crept in, edging out some of the ease I'd been feeling.

"Okay, Torren's taken care of. For now." Cal's voice still held a hint of good humor and I didn't want to ruin it for him. I wiped hurriedly at the tears pooling in the corners of my eyes, refusing to let them fall. Instead, I opted for distraction.

"Hey, Cal? I'm wondering something."

He settled onto the stool next me, elbows propped on the countertop. "What's that?"

"My dad cutting us off, from Below. Does that mean that the bond between me and Torren is severed? Did this fix him?" I didn't miss the note of hope in my voice as I spoke.

Surprise darted across his face, followed by what I knew to be sadness. "I'm sorry, Laney. The bond can't be severed that way. If it could, I think Angus would've done that the very first time it happened."

I nodded, understanding flashing through me. Thinking about the first bond I'd accidentally forged and the damage it had done to the man who'd been unlucky enough to be connected to me, I knew he was right. One date with me and Brett's life had been ruined. He'd hurt others as a result. Killed people. I'd found him and ended his life, using my magic in a way I'd sworn I never would. But it had been the only way to stop him and save someone else. I still carried the guilt of that within me. The lives lost because of me could never be forgotten. "I guess nothing's ever that easy. Is it?"

"Nothing that matters, at least." He laid a hand on my shoulder, fingers digging into the muscles there expertly. I tipped my head away, allowing him easier access to areas that were tight, stiff from everything that had gone on last night. And from sleeping on the couch, no doubt. He leaned closer, bringing his other hand up to join in the work and I moaned a little at how lovely it felt.

There was a heat building up between us, a tangible warmth flowing into my body. I recognized the sensation from when he'd healed me before. I relaxed into that feeling, indulging myself for a moment. Then, I gasped, jerking away from his touch, my eyes flying open.

"You're healing me right now." I spat the words, my skin prickling as betrayal flared through me. "You're using magic on me."

Cal flinched and that movement confirmed my sudden suspicion. I might be without my magic right now. Moose too. But Cal had his. He was the only one of us who did.

I slid off the stool and backed away from him. My heart pounded in my chest as I watched him, the way he couldn't make eye contact with me. Fear took hold in my gut, a dark voice in my mind whispering that I'd trusted too easily. That I was a stupid fool.

Cal stayed where he was, not coming after me, letting the distance separating us grow until I stopped moving. The silence between us went taut, the air in the apartment heavy with tension. When he finally raised his gaze to meet mine, I was struck by the brightness, the unworldly glitter in it. My father's eyes held flames sometimes, evidence of who he was. There was none of that in the depths of Cal's eyes. Instead, I was reminded of a night sky, stars spread out to infinity.

He spoke first, his words calm and even. "I never told you I didn't have my magic, Laney. I didn't lie to you."

I waited, expecting more of an explanation, but he gave me nothing else. Anger surged in me, replacing the fear I'd been feeling. "You knew that's what I thought. You had to know." My hands curled into fists as I threw the words at him. "The fact is, you didn't tell me."

"You're right, I didn't. But I did tell you we needed to talk."

The simple truth of those words struck a chord, ringing through me. But still, that dark voice reared up, beating back the calm logic of what he said, anger maintaining its foothold. *"He's hiding something from you."*

I shook my head, trying to shrug off the confusion that

filled me as the conflicting feelings warred with each other. The lack of control frightened me. Control had ruled my life, kept others safe from me. Feeling my grasp on it slip was terrifying.

"Laney, what's wrong?" Cal slid off the stool, taking a step toward me, but I held up my hand, needing him to stop. He did, allowing the space between us to remain as it was, concern on his face as he waited.

The silence between us stretched, stiff and heavy with tension, as I fought against the panic that was surging up in my chest. I took deep breaths, focusing on slowing the pounding beat of my heart. When I felt like I had regained some measure of composure, I focused on Cal once again.

"I need to know, Cal. Why would he cut me off and not you?" Saying the words made this newest betrayal even more real, an ache spreading through my chest at the thought that my father had chosen someone else over me.

He sighed. "Because my power is not his to take." The words were soft, almost a whisper, yet the magnitude of them hit me hard.

"Wait, what?" I asked. "What is that supposed to mean?"

Cal gestured toward the couch and when I didn't object, he made his way over to it and settled into one of the corners. He didn't say anything else, waiting for me to join him. I hesitated, trying to gauge how much I truly trusted him. A whine brought my head around. Moose had come in, worry written on his small face as he looked back and forth. He might not be able to communicate with us directly at the moment, but he was clearly aware of what was happening.

My need for answers finally won out over my fear. The fact that I was afraid of Callum was disturbing, this man who'd never hurt me, who had done everything he could to help me when needed. I wondered at how the seeds of mistrust had grown so quickly.

I squeezed myself into the opposite corner of the couch, pulling my knees up to my chest and wrapping my arms around them. Once settled, I focused my gaze on Callum and waited.

"What you know about me, what Angus told you, is limited." His voice was kind, almost gentle. "But I meant what I said. My power is not his to take."

"Then who can?" I asked, desperation underlaying my question. "Who are you?"

"It's not who I am, Laney. It's what." He paused, taking a deep breath before continuing. "I'm an angel."

It felt like the air had been sucked out of the room and we were now stranded in a vacuum. My pulse pounded in my ears as I stared at him, unsure what I could say.

"I know it's a shock."

A strangled sound left me, an attempt at laughter possibly. "But how?" I asked. "I've seen your hair, the red in it. I thought . . ." I trailed off, thinking of the assumptions I'd made since we met.

"You weren't wrong," Cal said, answering my unfinished

question. "It was the mark of your father. Of the debt I owed him. But he didn't create me, he doesn't rule me."

"You're an angel," I whispered, my thoughts spinning. "On earth? Why would there be an angel here?"

His face changed, shifting from acceptance to what I instantly recognized as grief. "I was banished. During the war your father started, I refused to choose a side. I healed those who were hurt, no matter who they were. In the end, when it was over, I was punished. Wounded and exiled. It took a very long time for me to heal. Angus is the one who found me, sheltered me. Helped me find my way."

"And that is the debt you needed to repay. That's why you stayed with me." My voice was a dull monotone as the statements floated out of my mouth. I had to talk it through, trying to wrap my brain around Cal's revelation.

"I came to you because of the debt. I stayed with you because I wanted to."

"How can I trust that?" The words left me before the thought had fully formed.

"Is it so hard to believe, Laney? That I would want to stay with you?"

There was an ache under my rib cage as he asked that question, as I realized how desperately I wanted to believe what he was telling me.

Cal leaned forward, his hand outstretched on the cushion between us. "All you have to do is test the bond between us. That will tell you if I'm a liar. Or not."

I reached toward him, hesitating, my hand hovering above his open palm. "If I don't have my magic, how can I check the bond?"

"Like the one between you and Torren, our bond existed before your magic was cut off. It's still there. Focus and you'll be able to see it."

I took a deep breath, choosing faith over fear, and let my hand drop into his.

Heat flared instantly as our skin touched and a golden light began to pulse, a rose tint visible through the center of it as the light stretched, running between the two of us. I hummed a note, wondering if it would respond to the sound and was delighted when it pulsed brighter. The connection between us was beautiful, and, as I kept my eyes trained on it, it became clearer and clearer. There was no darkness shadowing it. No evidence of deception. Based on what I could see, Cal was telling the truth.

I pulled my hand back slowly, the visible evidence of the bond growing dimmer as our contact decreased. I sat back, relief thrumming through me. I smiled at Cal and he gave me one in return. The comfortable companionship between us was back.

"What the Hell?" Torren's voice, angry and hurt, echoed behind me and the good feelings that had begun to take root evaporated. "You're bonded to him now too?"

Chapter Twenty-Eight

THE EASY CAMARADERIE we'd reestablished disappeared, replaced by strain. The smile on Cal's face was wiped away, back to the blank expression he'd worn so often lately. Seeing that made me realize how much he'd been holding back in an effort to avoid increased tension in our household.

I stood up from the couch and turned, taking in Torren's stunned expression. He was shirtless, his hair wet and the spare pair of Cal's sweatpants low on his hips. He'd lost weight since he'd joined us, the drain of the bond and his own turmoil evident in the carved muscles and hollows that hadn't been there before.

"I'm sorry, Tor. There hasn't been a chance for me to tell you." I offered him the apology, not waiting for him to demand an explanation. "It happened at the barn, when my father attacked us."

His gaze was furious, darting between me and Callum. "Why? Why did you do this?"

I didn't have an answer to that, but Cal did.

"It was necessary, in the moment. To prevent Angus from using me against her. I did it to protect her. To protect all of us."

Torren looked to me. "Did you know he was planning to do this?"

The suspicion that coated his question hurt, but I still answered him honestly. "I was as surprised as you are. It wasn't planned, Tor. Like he said, it was something he felt he had to do. To keep us safe."

He ran his hands through his hair, his eyes dropping to the floor. Then, as if resigned to the facts, he said, "Fine." He left the room before I could say anything else.

Moose whined again, trotting after him but stopping short as the door to the bedroom closed in his face. There was a pulse of pain in my core, hurt and disappointment that I recognized came from Torren, echoing through our bond.

I sighed, dropping down onto the couch again, resting my head in my hands. He'd been doing better. Coping. I hated the thought that this might set him back. The idea of it made me tired all over again. I was responsible for so much, for so many I cared about. Doubt flickered in my mind, making me wonder if I was capable of taking care of the ones I had left.

"He's jealous." The words were soft, Cal simply stating a fact.

I looked up at him, surprised by the idea. "What do you mean?"

"The bond was something only the two of you had. It made him special. Different than me. Now, the balance of things has changed."

His assessment didn't feel wrong. "Is this more wisdom gained by reading countless romance novels, Cal?"

He gave me a grin, as if he understood I was trying to lighten the mood. "They've rarely steered me wrong over the years." He looked back at the closed door. "He'll get over it. Give him some time to process the news. He'll find a way through."

"You have more faith in these things than I do, you know."

He shrugged. "Not really. I just have more practice. You'll learn. I have faith in you." He gave me a careful hug, his arms closing around me for the first time in too long. He pressed a gentle kiss to my forehead, and I felt a warmth pulse between us, comfort flowing from him into me. Despite the stress of the last few minutes, I felt myself relaxing and I could breathe once again.

"Thank you," I said, almost without meaning to.

"No problem. Now we need to get ready to go. We can't stay here much longer."

I nodded, immediately regretting the absence of his touch as his arms dropped away from me. He was right, we should be moving on. I wanted to check in on my house, get a few things for the fight ahead. I had a distinct feeling my father wasn't done.

"We should probably stop in at Hazelwood and talk to Miss Tilly. She may have information she can share with us." I needed the distraction, something else to focus on other than the tension that had returned to our little group.

Cal agreed. "I can drop us right outside the town. We'll have to walk in. You okay with that?"

I gave him a grin. "A little walk never hurt anyone."

Chapter Twenty-Nine

WITHIN AN HOUR, we were all ready to go, gathered together in the living room of Cal's apartment one last time. Moose leaned in against my leg. I reached down to pet him, remembering when my hand brushed empty air that he was trapped in his smaller form for the time being. I knelt beside him, rubbing the soft fur below his ears.

"We're gonna be fine," I whispered to him, hoping to offer him some comfort. "I promise." I leaned in and dropped a kiss onto the top of his head. He thanked me with a lick to my hand as I stood up.

Cal gave us all a quick once-over. "Everyone ready? I'll get us as close to the ward stones outside Hazelwood as I can. There's plenty of trees around, so we should have some good cover. Still, we all need to be prepared for anything."

I nodded. Torren shrugged. Moose offered a short bark of acknowledgment. We were as ready as we could be.

Cal turned away from us, calling the portal with ease. It opened quickly, the pressure change making my ears hurt. He glanced over his shoulder, as if making sure we were all still there. Then he stepped forward, onto the silver bridge. Moose followed him. Torren looked to me and I gestured for him to follow next. I didn't mind going last. When I stepped into the portal, I didn't bother to look back. I rested my hand on the butt of my gun, holstered within easy reach and loaded once again with blessed bullets. The feel of it eased some of the pressure in my chest as we were pulled out of Cal's apartment. I emerged from the portal into a smoke-filled haze that blurred my vision and stung my eyes. I could hear the crackle of trees as they burned and the shouts of people I couldn't see. I twisted, trying to get my bearings. It was Moose who found me, emerging from the smoke. He nudged me in the calf, then trotted off in the direction I assumed we were supposed to go.

I followed him, staying close so I could keep his stubbed tail in view. As we cleared a stand of brush, the smoke swirled, clearing for an instant and I could see Callum and Torren crouched down beside each other. They were speaking quietly back and forth. As they caught sight of me, they stopped. Cal stood and came to me. His eyes serious, he said, "Hazelwood is burning."

I gasped at the idea. Then coughed as smoke burned my mouth and throat. When I could speak again, I asked, "How?"

He threw a look over his shoulder, as if checking to

make sure we were still alone. "It has to be your father. Or Newt. They would target Hazelwood, knowing you'd come here."

"But how would they get in?" I asked. "Miss Tilly had the whole town warded."

Cal shook his head. "I don't know. But who else would do this? This isn't a natural fire. It's too . . . angry."

I looked around us and considered his assessment. There was something, a feeling in the air. The sound of the fire intensified, like it was creeping closer. I had to agree, it felt angry.

"We have to stop this somehow." Desperation coated the words as they left my mouth. "We can't let anyone be hurt because of me."

"I know, but we have to find a way in first. And, we have to stay together." He gripped my hand tightly. "No running off on your own."

I met his eyes. "I swear. No running off."

Callum turned back to the rest of our group. "All right, guys, let's get moving. We've got plenty of work to do."

Moose yipped and came to me. Torren stood, wiping his hands on the back of his pants. "Let's go."

Chapter Thirty

WE MADE OUR WAY through the haze, Cal leading the way. For the first time, I felt vulnerable without my magic. I hadn't had it long, only the last few years, but it had become a part of me. I'd grown comfortable with it. I'd begun to rely on it. My hand slipped to where my gun was holstered, but I hesitated to pull it out. I didn't want to shoot someone if I didn't have to.

The sound of voices grew louder ahead, screams punctuated with growls. My stomach twisted in fear. I liked the people of this town. They'd accepted me without question when I'd first arrived. I hated to think of any of them being hurt.

We cleared a stand of trees and I froze at the scene before me. Humans were locked in battle with creatures that hissed and swiped at their opponents with razor sharp claws. Torren's shocked gasp told me he recognized them as well.

These were the same creatures that had attacked us in the desert. Why were they here?

Callum raised his hand into the air as he whispered, and his sword appeared. Flames raced along the edge and he spared us a quick glance before he charged out ahead, into the battle. I snagged a thick branch from the ground and followed him, swinging my weapon up and smashing it against the back of the first creature I came upon. The surprise impact wobbled the creature, but more importantly, it turned its attention on me instead of the human it had been locked in combat with. I stepped back, drawing the creature after me, allowing the person it had been fighting to get to his feet and limp away. I hoped he was able to get help.

The creature snarled at me and I returned my focus to it. I trusted Cal and Torren to take care of themselves. Moose too, even in his smaller form. I needed to deal with the danger in front of me.

As the demon came at me, I swung the branch one more time. The creature jumped back, and I dropped the limb, pulling my gun from its holster in a smooth movement. I sighted and pulled the trigger. The blessed bullet struck hard, the demon jerking with the impact as it collapsed to the ground, motionless as black fluid leaked from it. The scent Cal had identified in his apartment rose up. Once again, I was struck by the distinctive smell of brimstone gone bad.

I reclaimed my makeshift club and stepped over the

body, intent on finding my next target. Adrenaline rushed through me and a part of me thrilled at the possibility of hurting something else. I stopped, puzzled at the idea. I'd fought before, demons and other creatures, even people who were a threat. But I'd *never* enjoyed it. What was happening to me?

I swayed for a second, almost overwhelmed by the conflicting emotions sparking within me. Claws wrapping around my arm brought my focus back to the battle happening around me. The demon twisted, spinning me and I brought the branch up in time to block its other arm as it slashed down toward my face. I screamed, using the leverage the branch afforded me to shove the creature away before bringing my gun up and shooting it in the face. As it fell to the ground, my vision went red and I was already looking for my next victim.

I fought my way through a gauntlet of creatures. When the branch was knocked loose and I lost my grip, I pulled my knife from the custom sheath in my boot. There was something both terrifying and satisfying in seeing the light dim in the eyes of each creature I defeated. Whether it was due to a blessed blade or a bullet, it didn't matter. I could feel a change coming over me, the roots of it spreading deeper within me as each body fell at my feet.

I lost track of time. I thrilled as the fight continued, not wondering where my friends were, battling each opponent as they appeared. My training sessions with Cal had built up my endurance and improved upon the defenses I'd already had. I wasn't impervious to injury and there was a part of me that registered pain when the creatures made contact, their claws slashing through my skin in places. But the joy of hurting them back spiraled through me and I fought on.

Until strong arms wrapped around me from behind, ratcheting down and pulling me tight against a hard, muscled chest. Warmth pulsed through me, eroding my will to fight and pull away. The pounding of my heart began to slow, and my vision cleared, the red haze retreating.

"Calm yourself, Delaney." Cal's deep, rich voice whispered in my ear and I rested back against him. "We can't have you hurting anyone now. So please, take some deep breaths and come back to us."

I did as he asked, my eyes taking in the group that had gathered around the two of us. Torren was tending to someone on the ground. Moose stood between me and the humans who faced us, shock and anger evident on their faces.

As the rush of adrenaline retreated, I started to shake. Cal's arms, which had begun to loosen tightened again, comforting me instead of restraining this time. He held me close, supporting me until I felt in control again. I realized he'd used the bond between us to break through the haze I'd been fighting in. To return me to myself.

The crowd of people parted making way for a small woman to step through. She raked her eyes over me, then said, "You are late once again, Girl."

Chapter Thirty-One

WE WERE ESCORTED into the town of Hazelwood by a group of residents designated by Miss Tilly to get us to her shop, The Hedgerow. We were not to stop along the way. We were not to talk to anyone.

Torren limped next to me, his face creased with anger and pain. Moose and Callum walked side by side ahead of us. Moose glanced over his shoulder at me twice, his worried eyes searching my face. Each time I was able to hear Cal whisper something that made Moose face forward again. I felt cut off from the ones I'd grown the closest to in recent months. Sadness settled in me, weighing me down. It was hard to keep myself moving. But with the suspicious looks cast my way by the guards surrounding us, I didn't dare stop.

The woman Torren had been tending to on the ground when my focus had returned was Aften, Miss Tilly's granddaughter. She'd been on the receiving end of a punch I didn't even remember throwing. There was another group that had been detailed to stay with her until she was checked by the only doctor in Hazelwood. She was being carefully moved onto a stretcher as we were led away.

Upon reaching The Hedgerow, we were ushered inside, and the door shut behind us. Two men were left to stand guard outside, but I was certain the others were close by. The street outside was quiet, no sign of any of the townspeople out and about. I worried about what that meant.

I wandered the store, the scent of hand-crafted soaps and candles pleasant and soothing. Moose curled up on a rug near the back of the store, choosing a nap instead of being involved in the conversation I knew was coming.

Right on time, Torren started. "What the hell was that back there?"

I didn't answer, instead taking a seat in the dark corner. I'd had tea with Miss Tilly here before, but my familiarity with the space didn't ease my discomfort tonight.

"Are you going to answer me?"

Fury surged inside me and I gasped at the sensation, overwhelmed in the moment. I gripped the arms of the chair, my nails digging into the upholstery so deeply I was afraid I'd ruin the fabric.

"You need to calm down." Cal's reasonable tone broke through the tension building. I was surprised to see his attention was on Torren, not on me.

"I need to calm down?" Tor's shock was palpable. It

pulsed through me and I realized that the emotions I was dealing with weren't all my own. "I'm not the one who went on a rampage back there. She almost killed some of the people we were trying to help."

I watched the exchange between the two men, horror settling over me. "Wait, what do you mean I almost killed people? I don't remember that at all. I only remember the demons."

Callum turned to me, his gaze serious. "You weren't yourself. We called to you several times, but you didn't respond to us. That's why I had to physically restrain you."

I tried to calm myself, to subdue the fear building in me. "The people I hurt? Are they going to be okay?"

Cal nodded. "They should be. With some medical treatment. I worry the more difficult healing will be your relationship with the people of this town."

I looked away from him, knotting my fingers together tightly in my lap. "Miss Tilly. She's the only one who can help with that right now."

"And since you knocked out her granddaughter, she might not be so forgiving." Torren's comment made me flinch.

"At the same time, the fact that she had us brought here to wait bodes well." Callum's voice was calm, offering me some measure of comfort. "She's not a rash woman. She doesn't rush to judgment, unlike some others."

"I can't believe I did this." I dropped my head into my

hands, hiding my face as tears filled my eyes. "Why would I? This isn't like me at all."

"That's probably what we should talk about while we wait." Torren opened his mouth to say something, but Cal stopped him with a hand. "This is a problem we need to solve. We can't solve it without information." He waited, as if giving Tor a chance to offer his opinion at this time. Torren crossed his arms over his chest and gave Cal a tight nod.

Cal turned back to me. "Now, why don't we start with you telling us what you remember about the fight. We'll reconstruct everything as best we can. See where things went wrong."

I thought back to the battle, from the time we jumped into the fray to the very end when Cal's arms had wrapped around me. I told them what I could remember. It felt to me like I'd been fighting for a short period of time. When Cal explained it had taken us forty-five minutes to battle our way to the point where he'd had to stop me from hurting Aften further, shock settled in deep. I'd lost at least half an hour. How could this have happened?

"What was the last thing you remember before I grabbed you?" Cal asked.

I closed my eyes, envisioning the faces of the demons I'd fought against. They were identical, one after the other, nothing to distinguish between them. As they fell, there seemed to be another one to fight every time I turned around. I switched my focus to the way I'd felt during the battle. There hadn't been fear or even anger, but there had been a sense of satisfaction as I'd watched the creatures die. The realization horrified me.

"I enjoyed it. I actually enjoyed killing them all." The words left me before I'd thought it all the way through. I looked to Cal, desperation making me ask, "What in all the Hells is wrong with me?"

He knelt next to my chair, taking my hand in his. Shock made me shiver so I leaned toward the warmth he radiated. He studied my eyes and I forced myself to remain still under his scrutiny. I could feel my skin tingling where his fingers wrapped around mine. Heat began to spiral through me as we sat there, the physical connection between us amplifying the internal one Callum was exploring.

The temperature coursing through me amped up and I gasped as his energy filled me, stretching me from the inside out. Then suddenly it was gone. Cal's hand had slipped from mine and I was terribly aware of how lonely I felt without the contact between us. "Please, don't leave me." My voice cracked as a sob filled my throat. I didn't want to be alone.

His hand drifted up to my cheek and rested there for a moment, a reassuring touch I didn't want to end. "You're going to be okay. I promise."

The door opened, the little bell attached to it ringing through the store and breaking the moment between us. Miss Tilly walked in, her presence demanding our attention. "Girl," she called out. "Let me see you."

Chapter Thirty-Two

I LEFT THE COMFORTABLE corner I'd been waiting in and came to where she stood. Miss Tilly was a small woman, but her presence was immense. There was a sense of gravity about her no matter where she went. Things orbited around her. And no one doubted she was strong enough to keep everything in its place.

As I came to a stop in front of her, she placed both palms on my cheeks, tipping my chin down and gazing deep into my eyes. We stood like that as seconds stretched into minutes before she released me. I stumbled back as she broke contact with me and recognized Torren's grip on my arm, stabilizing me.

Miss Tilly shot a look at Callum. "She's lost her tether." She didn't say anything else, and headed to the back of the store, away from the front windows where prying eyes might peer in if they dared.

Cal nodded, following her. "I felt the same when I checked her before you arrived." He took a deep breath, glancing at me over his shoulder. "Is it because her mother is gone?" His voice was low, but I still heard him. "Or because of Angus?"

Miss Tilly stopped at a table in the darkest corner of her store. I hadn't seen it on my previous trips there and wondered if it was a new addition or if I had somehow missed it. She pulled open a drawer on the front, taking something from it before making her way to the area where I'd been waiting before. She sat in her regular chair, tipping her head toward the one next to it as if indicating I should sit next to her.

As I sat down, I said, "Miss Tilly, I'm so sorry. I didn't mean to hurt anyone."

She patted me on the arm. "We all have mistakes, Girl. Aften will learn from this as well. But your apology is well meant and appreciated."

She then leaned over and blew into the cradle made by her palms. "Girl, give me your hand."

I did as I was told, having been well trained by my previous interactions with the leader of Hazelwood. I reached out my right hand, holding it open. Miss Tilly pressed what she held into the center of my palm, then closed my fingers tight around it. She squeezed hard and I tried not to fight against the pressure, even though sharp edges dug deep into my skin. When she finally let go, she said, "Open now."

I released my fingers from around the object. An indentation had been left on my skin and there were indeed cuts that welled with blood. But the crystal she'd given me flared bright white with light as soon as it was revealed. Then I watched as the light began to fade, darkness forming at the center with tendrils reaching out toward the points.

Miss Tilly examined it from where she sat. Finally, she said, "Her darkness is spreading."

Cal nodded, a grim look on his face. When no one else said anything in response, I felt the need to speak up. "Someone please tell me what's going on."

Cal looked around at the group assembled in Miss Tilly's store. Torren watched him from where he leaned against the wall, a stubborn set to his jaw as he observed everything that was happening. Miss Tilly cleared her throat and gave Callum a nudge as Moose whined from where he lay.

"Your tie to humanity, what Miss Tilly called your tether, it's been cut."

Chapter Thirty-Three

Cold rushed through me at his announcement. None of what he was saying made any sense. "But, I'm human. How could I lose that?"

Cal dropped down next to me, his eyes on my face. "This is what I've been able to figure out. Your mother being here, in the world, is what kept Angus, the father you knew all your life, in the human form he chose. Without her, he's lost his grip on the part that was allowing him to be human. He's reverted to his true form." I nodded as he spoke, remembering the fearsome sight of my father outside the barn as his human face disappeared and I saw him as he really was for the first time. "There's nothing anchoring the human part of you anymore. Your mother is gone and your father, he's chosen to let go. He's chosen darkness again."

"But what does that have to do with me? I'm not my father."

Miss Tilly patted my arm. "It's good you believe that. Like each one of us here, you are your own person. You have your own choices to make. You must be strong enough to make them, even when they hurt."

Choices. The word alone left me weary, a bone aching tiredness that threatened to swamp me. "I'm clearly not good at making choices." My words sounded bitter, but I couldn't take them back.

"Don't be silly, Girl. We have no time for silly. You make the best choices you can, like everyone else in the world does. Then, you learn."

"But if people are hurt along the way, that must mean I've made the wrong choice."

Miss Tilly shook her head at my comment. "These are the moments when I remember how young you still are." She sighed before she continued. "There are times when people will be hurt, no matter the choice you make. You still have to decide."

The look on her face was so full of pain, I had to wonder what had happened in her past. But I couldn't ask her those kinds of questions now. I needed to focus on the problem at hand. "How do I keep this from getting worse? You said the darkness is spreading. Can I stop it?"

Miss Tilly assessed me for a moment before giving me a short, decisive nod. "You can slow it down. You can limit its reach. But, it's a part of you, something you must learn to live with."

She stood up, her attention turning to the two men who were always with me. "You both are part of this now. The bonds can help as much as they can hurt. Help her learn. Help her manage."

Taking that as a signal we were supposed to go, I asked one final question. "The demons we fought tonight, did they make it into Hazelwood?"

Miss Tilly grinned, a ferocious smile that bared her teeth. "The magic here is old and strong. Evil will have to work much harder to break through than it did tonight."

"Why didn't you wait them out in town?" Torren asked. "If they couldn't get in here, why risk casualties if everyone was safe?"

"I'm still the leader here, and you're still rude, Boy." The tone in her voice allowed for no argument. "We are not cowards, hiding from battles we must fight. Our people were attacked as they returned home. They did their part to save something valuable, we did our part to save them."

I wondered at what she was saying. It didn't surprise me that the people of this town would fight to rescue their own. "Wait, what do you mean they saved something valuable?" It felt like the answer to that question was important.

Miss Tilly turned shining eyes to me, and my heart skipped a beat. "Oh, Girl, I'm sorry. Your home. The demons burned down your home."

Chapter Thirty-Four

Callum's arms caught me as my legs went weak. A comforting warmth spiraled from him into my center, lending me a portion of his strength and resolve. His reassurance beat back the sadness that had overwhelmed me when I'd heard Miss Tilly's words. My home, the one I'd built on my own, was gone.

"It's been destroyed before, you know. Rebuilt stronger each time." I looked to Miss Tilly and the kindness on her face filled my heart. I knew it had been her home too, years before it had been mine. But I'd promised her I would take care of it.

I offered her what I could in this moment. "I'll do everything I can to restore it to the way it was. I swear."

Miss Tilly nodded, then dusted her hands together. "I must go. Aften needs checking. No one here will bother you now. Be safe." With that, she was gone, and we were alone in her store once again.

Cal had followed Miss Tilly as she exited through the front door and was surveying the street. Torren remained where he was, his arms still folded tightly across his chest, as if he could hold all his feelings inside with that simple gesture. The trouble was, his emotions were pouring into me through the bond and I had no way of shielding myself from them with my magic gone. I watched him from where I sat, wondering how and when to bridge the gap between us.

It was Callum who gave us the opportunity. He called to Moose, who jumped up from where he'd been napping. "Guys, we need some transportation. Moose and I are going to see if we can find someone willing to give us a ride. We'll be back." He shot me a serious look before he turned and left the store, quiet descending after the door had closed.

I took a deep breath and made the first move. "Okay, we clearly need to talk." Trusting my legs to hold me now, I stood up and walked over to where he leaned against the wall. I kept a reasonable bit of distance between us, instead propping myself up against the sales counter next to him. Tor didn't say anything, keeping his narrowed eyes trained on me. "So, let's do this. Talk."

I met his gaze and waited. Silence stretched between us, but I didn't move to break it. This was all up to him. Tor finally shrugged, breaking eye contact with me as he dropped his gaze to the floor. He sighed and ran his hand through his hair, drawing attention to how long it had gotten since we'd first met.

"You're tough on me, sometimes." The words were soft, but it was a start.

"What do you mean?" I tried to keep my response even, no aggravation or accusation in my tone.

He gestured at the space between us. "I mean, that didn't come out right. This thing between us. It's not easy for me to handle. I feel … ," he paused, looking up to the ceiling before finally returning his attention to me. "I feel very out of control."

That I understood. "I don't like feeling that way either, you know."

He nodded. "But usually I can find a solution. With this, there isn't one. And then I find out that you have a bond with him now too. That makes everything even harder."

I didn't offer a response, even though I wanted to. There were plenty of things I wanted to say to him. To remind him that our bond had been an accident. That I'd never wanted to hurt him. That this was as difficult for me to handle as it was for him. But he needed time to vent. It was my time to listen. I owed him that as his friend.

"I know I can't compete with Cal." The admission left him on a rush of breath. "But, for a little while, there was this one thing we had that was separate, that didn't include him. Now even that's been taken away."

I waited, sure there was something else. Torren began to pace, his shoes tapping out a rhythm on the wood floors as he worked up to what he needed to say. It was difficult for me to stay silent. I dug my nails into the palm of my hand as I watched him.

"I had a life, you know. Before all this happened." He took a deep breath. "I've told myself that this is my fault. That I should never have followed you from Angel Falls. I should've let it go. But I couldn't. Not then. And not now."

"I'm sorry." It wasn't enough, but it was true. He looked at me, his eyes bright. "I'm sorry for all of this. That you felt the need to follow me, to solve the mystery. Part of that is because of who you are but my magic is just as much to blame. I used magic on you, that first night. When you interviewed me. I tried to keep it small, controlled, but I didn't know as much about my magic then. It was a mistake. I wish I could take it back."

I didn't see any surprise on his face at my admission. He assessed me for a long moment, before he crossed the distance between us. He reached down, lightly wrapping his fingers around mine. I'd avoided contact with him as much as possible since our fateful kiss. He had done the same. "When I left, it took everything I had to walk away from you. And I know you won't believe this, but it did get easier, bit by bit, the further away I got. It wasn't pleasant, but it was manageable. I didn't come back to you because I had to. I came back because I wanted to."

With that, he leaned down and kissed me again, one gentle press of his lips against mine. Instead of desire or passion coming through the bond with that contact, I instead felt loneliness and a deep longing. Then he stepped back and released my hand, the emotions easing in intensity as the distance between us increased once again. I realized I'd been holding my breath and it left me in a rush.

"I'm afraid I don't know how to do this," I whispered, and he nodded in understanding. "I don't want anyone to get hurt."

"You told me before, there couldn't be anything between us other than the bond. Because I wasn't free to choose. But I'm telling you, I did choose. I chose to come back to you."

The front door of the store opened, the bell above it ringing out, louder than it seemed possible. Cal looked back and forth between the two of us. "Did you manage to work some of this out?" he asked.

Torren shrugged and headed for the door. He patted Cal on the shoulder as he passed him. "I said what I had to say." Then he stepped outside onto the street and the door closed behind him.

Cal turned his attention to me. "You all right?"

I shook my head. "I don't know. I feel too young and too old all at the same time. If that makes any sense."

He offered me his standard grin, the one that quirked up a corner of his mouth and made his eyes shine. "I get that. If it helps, I feel the same way. I'm old but at the same time, I'm still learning how to manage in this world."

"You don't have to be nice to me, you know." I held up a

hand as he prepared to offer what I was sure would be a sarcastic comment. "Never mind. We have places to go. Did you actually find us a car to drive?"

He nodded, opening the door for me as I walked toward him. "I did. Seemed as good an excuse as any other to give you two time to chat about your feelings. You can take your frustration out on the road and I can save my energy in case we need to portal our way somewhere."

He snagged me in a quick hug as I reached him, his body keeping the door open. His grip this time was gentle, reassuring, and I soaked up the strength of him before he let me go. I stepped out of the store and saw Moose, his head hanging out of the passenger side rear window as he waited for us to join him in the car Callum had borrowed.

"All right then. I'm driving." I held my hand out and Cal dropped the keys into my palm as he walked by.

"I'll make sure to wear my seatbelt," was his only response.

Chapter Thirty-Five

When we pulled up the long gravel driveway to my home, I fought back the anger swelling in my chest at the sight of what remained. The front porch was almost completely gone, charred black timbers visible in some places. The roof had collapsed on the front and the right, the windows blown out. I circled around it, the car's headlights catching on different areas of damage as I slowly assessed what had been done. Miss Tilly had been right, it was badly damaged. But it wasn't irreparable.

The separate building I'd used as a garage appeared almost untouched. I pulled to a stop in front of it and we all got out. I went to the side door and twisted the handle, which turned easily. Someone had left it unlocked, waiting for me to return.

I pushed it open and stepped inside, ignoring Cal's cautionary whisper to let him go first. I slid to the side and hit the switch. Light flooded the space, leaving nowhere for enemies to hide.

The car Angus had left in my care, the sleek red Mustang he'd loved, sat in its regular spot. There wasn't a spot on it. The same wasn't true of the other vehicle that shared the garage. My car, the purple Hellcat Angus had teased me about so many times, had clearly been the target of someone's rage. Claws had raked along the panels, down into the metal beneath the paint. One of the doors had been torn off and lay nearby on the garage floor. The seats were shredded, pieces of broken glass glinting in the light from above.

"It's only a car," I whispered to myself as I walked around it. "It doesn't really matter."

Torren surprised me, his voice unexpected as I hadn't realized he'd followed me in with Cal. "Don't lie to yourself, Laney. We all know how much this car meant to you."

I nodded and looked away from him, wiping furiously at my eyes. After everything else that had happened, it seemed silly to cry about a car. But I was so tired of losing pieces of my life. This felt like one thing too many.

Callum stood across from me, the purple hood between us. He gave the car an appraising look. "I'm sure that's fixable. A few hours to bang out the dents and a little paint, should be good as new." He said it with a completely straight face, but there was a teasing tone in his voice that made me laugh despite how I was feeling.

Torren chimed in. "In fact, I'd bet we could find a couple

high school kids who could get this done in no time. Their first fixer upper."

I shook my head at the two of them, surprised and warmed by their joint effort to make me feel better. Maybe it was the absence of my other magic, but I was more aware of the bonds I shared with them. The connections felt almost tangible when I focused my attention on the magical threads running between us. I resisted the urge to reach out and strum my fingers across them. Instead, I didn't fight the waves of comfort that were sent my way and allowed them to wash over me, easing some of the hurt and fear I'd been overwhelmed by.

Moose crawled out from under a bench in the corner and the sight of the stub of his tail wiggling so happily made me grin. He'd found a stash of treats I'd hidden there, and the bag hadn't been much of an obstacle. He'd ripped right into it and scarfed them down. A shiny strip of the bag was stuck to his fur and he pawed at it until it came loose, fluttering to the ground. He gave me his widest doggie grin and let out a huge belch before laying down to observe us, his front paws crossed over each other. Clearly, as far as Moose was concerned, all was not lost.

"Where do we go from here?" Torren asked, bringing me back to the situation at hand. "We need some place secure that won't be high on anyone else's list."

I didn't have any ideas to contribute on that note, but I had something I needed. "I've gotta find myself some clothes too." The sweatpants I wore were covered in demon ichor and there were also spots of what I suspected was human blood. "And another shower would be nice," I added at the idea of what was likely trapped in my curly hair.

Cal gave us all a look. "Immediate needs. Food, shelter and clothing. We need to get the car back to Hazelwood. I promised we'd return it tonight. We'll brainstorm from there."

Moose trotted to the open door, sticking his nose out and giving the air an exploratory sniff. When he turned and gave us a bark over his shoulder, we all interpreted that as a sign it was safe for us to leave the garage. Even then, Cal insisted on being in front of me with Torren bringing up the rear.

Nothing stirred as we exited. I made sure the door was shut tight and locked before we continued to the car. We piled in, Moose and I in the back seat this time. Callum and Torren both scanned the open area around where we'd parked before they took the front seats.

"Should I assume the fact that you don't want to drive is a sign you've finally realized you're a terrible driver? Or is this a sign of some devastating illness you haven't told us about yet?" Cal's grin was obvious in the rear-view mirror. I didn't answer, tossing him the key as I settled back in my seat. Moose laid down beside me and my hand dropped to his back. I stroked the line of gray fur that ran along his spine and smiled when he gave a contented sigh.

Cal started the car and turned it back toward the gravel

drive. I resisted the urge to watch the home I'd made disappear, so I kept my eyes resolutely on my window, refusing to look back. As the bushes marking the end of the property line began to get larger, Cal sped up, intent on getting us to the highway as quickly as he could. There was a hint of strange movement among the leaves. I leaned in toward the glass, my breath fogging it up for a second.

"Slow down!" I called out the warning, but it was too late. Demons swarmed from the brush lining both sides of the gravel road. Bodies hit us from the right side first and I screamed at the sound of breaking glass. Hands tipped with stiletto sharp claws reached in through the opening, straining toward me. Moose threw himself at them, sinking his teeth into the skin and latching on. Black blood sprayed and I heard shrieks from outside. I pulled my knife and slashed at a demon that had somehow found enough purchase on the side of our moving vehicle that he was trying to crawl into the back seat. The seat belt I'd habitually put on hampered my movement, so I slipped my hand under it to free up my range of motion. The demon hissed at me, the yellow slits of its eyes on my face before it lunged. I didn't try to stop its attack, twisting quickly to the side so its teeth missed my throat. Its claws sank into the meat of my stomach, the searing pain hot and bright. I tightened my grip on the knife and before it could adjust its angle and snap at me again, I stabbed it in the side of the head.

The demon didn't even have a chance to cry out. Its eyes

went wide and then it sagged against me. The smell of it was overpowering and I forced myself not to gag. I tried to push the creature off me but the dead weight of it was more than I expected. I closed my eyes as a wave of nausea hit me. Moose gave a concerned whine next to me, nudging my open hand with his nose. I could feel the car was still moving, cold air streaming in around us as Cal pushed the car to go even faster.

When the tires hit pavement, there was a sudden jolt and Cal twisted the wheel hard left. My stomach rolled with the movement and I groaned. Torren's voice pulled my attention away from how bad I felt as he demanded I stay awake. "Look at me, Laney. Damn it, open your eyes and look at me."

I did as I was told, even offering what I hoped was a brave smile. I swallowed against the lump of bile in my throat. "I'm not dead. Just about to puke from the smell back here."

Callum whispered something that sounded like a curse and Torren offered his own version. The demon's body slithered over me as Cal jerked the wheel suddenly, another tight turn, and I flinched at the thought that this thing might still be alive.

The car's engine roared as Callum accelerated even more, and I had to wonder if the demons were chasing after us even on the highway. His eyes met mine in the mirror and he held my gaze for a fraction of a second before returning his focus to the road.

As the outskirts of Hazelwood came into view, hope filled me. Once we made it past the stones that warded the town, we would be safe. The car shot forward and I knew Cal would make sure we got through. Moose snuggled closer to me now that we were no longer under immediate attack and I rested my hand on his back.

"Hells," said Cal from the front seat. I leaned around so I could see through the front window. Demons had spilled across the road in front of us, blocking our way to the safety that had been so close. "They were waiting for us."

It made sense. Going to check out my house had been something Angus would've expected me to do. The demons he'd stationed there were the first wave of attack. This group was the fallback team. He'd known we would run back to Hazelwood if we survived the attack at home.

"Hold on." Instead of slowing down like I expected, Cal hit the gas, pushing the pedal down to the floor. The engine roared in response, the force as we jumped forward pushing me back into the seat. I wrapped my arms around Moose, holding him close to keep him safe.

I closed my eyes as we hit the first line of demons, their screams and the sound of metal buckling loud in my ears with every impact. The car jolted over bodies and the shrieks outside grew louder. With every hit, it felt like we were slowing down.

Torren cursed as glass shattered around him. "Don't stop, Cal. Whatever happens, don't stop." Claws scraped along the door, the sound making me shudder.

I screamed as the face of one of the demons appeared in Torren's window. It reached through for him, wicked claws sinking into his arm and tugging him toward the opening. Moose jumped up from the back seat, snarling. I shoved the demon body off me and released my seat belt. I threw myself forward, reaching around the seat and grabbed Torren to keep him in place. The demon growled and leaned back, its feet braced against the metal of the door shell, using that leverage to pull Tor out of his seat. My grip slipped and I reached for him again. My hand landed on his injured shoulder and he grunted with pain, but I refused to let him go this time.

"Hang on, everybody. We're almost there." Cal's voice was strained, his usual calm fractured. I tightened my hold on Torren as we were suddenly airborne, launched from the last hill right before the entrance to Hazelwood. The demon that clung to the side of the car shrieked as we crossed the boundary line of the magic guarding the town. The demon's skin flared, and sparks danced across it until it finally exploded.

The car hit the ground with jarring force and Cal slammed on the brakes. We slid and spun, coming to a rest sideways in the middle of the highway that carved the town of Hazelwood in two.

Chapter Thirty-Six

Miss Tilly didn't seem surprised by our frantic arrival. She came to where the car sat, steam rising from the hood as we tried to calm our desperate breathing. A group of people followed her. They helped us get the doors open and supported us as we made our way free. Aften was there as well, issuing instructions on how best to examine and care for our wounds.

My knees went weak as I looked at the car, the gouges in the metal panels proof of how sharp those grasping claws had been. As was his way, Moose was there, his warmth pressing against the side of my leg. Having him next to me, I swallowed against the lump in my throat. He had become a constant in my life. One I knew would be devastating to lose.

I crumpled to the ground, the energy to hold myself up exhausted. I wrapped my arms around Moose's neck and pulled him close. The smell of him was comforting, that unique canine scent that followed him everywhere.

He let me hold him like that, unmoving, until I finally released him. He licked my cheeks and nose until I met his eyes. There was a deep knowing look in them, as if somehow, he knew everything that truly mattered in this world, and would tell me the answers if I asked.

"You're the best Hound," I whispered to him, his ears perking up at my voice. "The very best I could ever have."

He licked my cheek again and then turned his head at the sound of Cal calling his name. He looked to me, as if asking permission. I waved him away. "Go on then. He must need you."

I watched as he trotted away, his stubbed tail ticking back and forth. Moose was replaced by Anita, the owner of the town's diner, and a trio of people intent on checking me for injuries that needed treating. I refused their offers to help me up even though it was a struggle to get to my feet alone. They escorted me to the bed and breakfast in town. The owner, Donna Kay, had earlier set aside space where the people injured defending Hazelwood could be examined and treated. The fact that she was willing to allow us to be treated there as well warmed my heart. She was the boss within the confines of these walls, her ownership evident as she directed volunteers. She'd always been kind to me, and the idea I might lose that along with everything else made my heart clench.

The smile on her face when she saw me was open and welcoming. Her hands hovered over me as she stopped herself in the act of trying to pull me in for a hug. Even though it went against her natural instincts, she was careful to respect my boundaries. I had always tried to limit contact with humans, afraid I'd lose control and feed on them. Or worse, accidentally create a bond like I had with Torren. But I wouldn't have minded a hug right now.

"Well, you've gone and gotten yourself torn up again it looks like." There was no recrimination in her voice, no admonishment. Only maternal concern. "Don't worry, sweetheart, we'll get you taken care of." I dimly heard her giving instructions about what room to put me in and ordering one of the women close by to sit with me until Donna Kay came to relieve her. "Let her be as much as you can. She needs some rest after all this mess."

Chapter Thirty-Seven

I DON'T REMEMBER how long I was there. True to Donna Kay's prediction, I did need some rest and sleep overcame me quickly. I had vague dreams, hard to remember. It felt as if I was floating, apart from myself, drifting with a current outside my control. The scenes kept shifting, but there was this constant feeling that I was alone, cut off from all that mattered to me. That I would never find my way back. Everything I reached for slipped through my hands and I couldn't keep myself from being swept away, overwhelmed by the waves of force pushing me along, until I was drowning, unable to break free.

I woke with a gasp, anxiety spiking, and that dark voice was back, whispering in my mind words I couldn't fully make out. My heart sped at the sound of it though, that voice making me question my sanity again. I didn't want to listen to it. I didn't want to know what it was trying to tell me. I looked around the darkened room, surprised that I was alone. I sat up quickly, making my head swim. My lips were dry, and I ached for a drink of water.

I reached for the lamp on the nightstand, needing to see what was around me. "Hells, it'd be a handy thing to see in the dark," I joked out loud to myself.

"It would."

The voice jolted through me, surprise that I wasn't alone as I'd thought. My heart beat a rapid rhythm as panic threatened and I felt defenseless for a moment.

"It's just me, Laney."

With those words, recognition sank in and I knew that voice. It was tired. It was rough.

"Damn it all, Cal," I said, my voice shaky. "You scared me."

He turned the lamp on with a flick and light flooded around us. He slumped in the chair, exhaustion and pain stamped all over him.

"How're you feeling?" He leaned forward, elbows on his knees as he scrubbed his hands across his face.

I sat up, propping myself up against the headboard. The skin across my stomach felt tight and tender with every movement. I lifted my shirt and saw the pink lines that marked the place where claws had dug in.

"How long did it take you to heal me? Was it bad?"

"Not the worst I've ever had."

"I've still got all my clothes on so that's a good sign, I guess."

Cal gave a tired laugh. "Depends on how you look at it. But you're probably right."

His voice trailed off, silence settling over us. I waited, my skin itching with the need to say something, but I kept quiet. Whatever it was, he'd tell me when he was ready. I played with the edge of my shirt, the torn hem snagging on my rough and broken fingernails. The back and forth was hypnotic, a soothing distraction.

"He's gone." His words were so quiet, I almost missed them.

I stopped tugging at the loose strings I'd pulled free from the fabric. "Wait, who's gone?" Fear settled in my gut, my stomach twisting.

Cal looked at me, his gaze intense even in the dim light of the room, and there was a frightening finality in his voice. "Torren. He's gone. We can't find him anywhere."

Chapter Thirty-Eight

"How could he just disappear?" Worry made me want to act, to run out of the room Donna Kay had graciously let me rest in. I reached out for him, testing the bond, but there was no response. Not even a flicker. It was shut down. Cut off. "He promised he wouldn't leave again. He promised me."

Callum scrubbed his hands through his hair, the gesture emphasizing how tired he was. "I don't think he went willingly, Laney."

"What do you mean?"

"He was with a group, searching for some of the locals who were missing. They heard someone calling for help. It was right at the edge of town and, when they started back, they realized Torren wasn't with them. It looks like he was taken."

Taken. The impact of that vibrated through me and

nausea swelled in my throat. Anyone who would have taken Tor wouldn't have good things planned for him.

I forced myself to be calm, taking deep breaths to bring my heart rate back down. The pounding in my head eased and I almost began to feel in control once again.

Then that dark voice whispered in my head. *He's not worth your worry. He's weak. He's always been weak.* I shook it off, unwilling to follow that train of thought.

Instead I said what I knew to be true. "They'll hurt him to hurt me." The words tasted bitter as I said them, the truth a heavy weight to carry. A part of me was afraid whoever took him would kill him. Another part of me was afraid they wouldn't.

"We'll find him, Laney."

I nodded. "I know we will. But will it be too late when we do?"

Chapter Thirty-Nine

I DIDN'T SLEEP the rest of the night, despite Cal's request that I at least try. Every time I closed my eyes, I saw Tor's face, creased with pain. I could hear his voice, screaming my name in agony and sometimes, even hatred.

Miss Tilly and her granddaughter, Aften, were the leaders of the town's defense. They directed everyone to where they needed to be, no one questioning them or daring to disagree. When the sheriff arrived, she and Miss Tilly secreted themselves in The Hedgerow. Rumors spread quickly that deputies had been attacked by creatures lurking in the shadows. And that people in other communities, those without the protections Hazelwood had already in place, were missing.

Frustration welled up within me. There was no doubt we were the cause of what was happening around us. The peace of this community, and those around it, had been broken because of me. We had to find some way to make this right.

※

WE GATHERED AT THE Hedgerow to discuss our next steps.

"Is there anyone who'd be willing to help us search for Torren?" My voice was tired, but I hoped the fear in it wasn't noticeable. I didn't want to, but I'd beg for help if necessary.

Miss Tilly watched me, her eyes assessing everything as always. I didn't say anything else, the quiet blanketing the store.

"We've already lost enough." Aften spoke into the silence. "We can't afford to help you any more than we already have."

"Is that really your decision to make?" Cal asked, stepping up beside me. I appreciated the show of support but worried as the tension surrounding us ramped up. "Shouldn't that be something the people here get to decide for themselves? Whoever took Torren is the same person who attacked the town earlier. Finding Torren means finding the one responsible."

"It's not worth the risk." Aften's eyes flashed, her fists clenching at her sides. For the first time since I'd met her, her calm exterior slipped away, frustration and anger palpable in the air.

Moose growled from his place near the front door of the shop. A knock followed a moment later.

Aften threw an angry glance at me before she went to answer. Cal's hand found mine, his fingers squeezing tight as reassurance thrummed between us. I offered him a shaky smile in return, a silent thank-you.

Low voices passed back and forth as we waited. I was surprised to see Anita waiting outside. She seemed insistent on joining us in the store, something held tightly in her hand.

Aften finally stepped aside, allowing Anita entrance. The older woman made her way directly to Miss Tilly, her posture stiff and straight. Even though it had been a long night, she didn't seem tired. I wondered at how she kept going.

Miss Tilly led Anita away from where we stood, over into the corner of the store. Their backs to us, I could hear their whispered voices but none of what was actually said between them. Miss Tilly finally nodded and as if that was the signal, Anita turned and walked past us, her eyes lifting to mine only briefly in acknowledgment. Then the door closed behind her.

I waited, impatient but understanding that speaking out of turn wouldn't improve matters for any of us. I chewed on my bottom lip instead.

When Miss Tilly gave a sigh loud enough to be heard across the store, dread wormed through my stomach. She turned and looked to me, the sadness in her eyes clear even from where I stood. She crossed the distance between us, and I forgot to breathe in that time as I waited for her.

"This is meant for you." Her hand was extended, a folded piece of white paper held out to me. My name was written in block letters on it, but I didn't take it from her. I stared at it, my hands beginning to shake.

Callum reached for it instead. I didn't miss the glance he threw my way, the worry reflected in his stance. The paper rustled as he opened it, his eyes scanning what it contained. His lips hardened into a thin line as he read. When he was done, he offered the note to me. I shook my head.

"Just tell me. What does it say?"

He nodded in response, not forcing the issue. "Exactly what you thought. Torren's alive. For now. But only if you agree to exchange yourself for him. Tonight."

"That's it? There's nothing else in there?" My voice was barely a whisper.

"They want you to come alone, of course." I lifted my eyes from the floor, focusing on him. "Which isn't going to happen. We won't even discuss that."

"If that's what it takes to save him, then I have to do it."

"It's not negotiable, Delaney. You're not going without me and Moose. Not this time. We won't let you." His words were firm, steel running beneath them.

My breathing was shaky, my head starting to swim at the idea of what was happening to Torren as we talked about this. How much pain was he in as we debated our next step?

I shook my head, my hands out to keep Cal at a distance but he ignored them. He pushed them aside and pulled me to his chest, his arms wrapping me up and holding me close. His warmth leaked into me, soothing the frightened parts deep inside. The resolve I'd been clinging to since Torren had disappeared again fled, my legs going weak for a moment. I didn't fight against it and instead let Cal support me. I hid my face against his shoulder and breathed in the comforting scent that was uniquely his.

He whispered in my ear. "We'll get him back. I promise you." I didn't argue with him or try to pull away. He held me up and I chose to believe he was right.

Chapter Forty

THE CHAPEL WAS beautiful. From its vantage on the bluff, it overlooked the valley below. In the summer, the fields down there would be the vibrant green of growing things, wildflowers spreading through the untamed areas. The trees that stood sentry were leafless now, but in the span of months would be fully covered, the whole canopy filled with varying shades of green, like the first time I'd seen it. Tonight, the whole ridge was blanketed in snow, the surface unbroken. It had been sculpted into whirls and peaks by the almost constant wind. For the moment, that wind was distant, beating around the base of the bluff. The area around the chapel was still, silent. There was a sense of serenity wrapped around the building as I stood outside.

The lights inside glowed golden through the stained glass. It was a welcoming place under normal circumstances. Even though the fallen snow was pristine, unmarred by any tracks, I knew something waited inside for me. The message I'd received hadn't told me exactly what was going to happen, but I had an idea. I might be young, I might be stubborn, but I was still my father's daughter. Which meant I wasn't a fool. They'd taken something from me. I was here to get it back.

Cal's solid presence on the path I'd left behind lent me strength. I knew Moose walked with him. I'd told them both I was willing to face this threat on my own, even knowing I was without my magic. They'd refused, without hesitation. Whatever had to be done, I wasn't going to do it alone. Proof I could learn from my mistakes.

The wide doors opened easily when I pulled on the handles. Candles glittered inside, reflecting off the golden fixtures that ringed the building. Pews were arranged at an angle on both sides of a central aisle, pointing the way to the raised dais at the front of the church. The altar stood, draped in white. Torren lay unmoving at the base, propped up facing me as I made my way forward. Blood coated his arms and the side of his face. Fear wove through me and I reached for the bond between us. It had been silent since he'd been taken. I hoped that since he was here, right in front of me, whatever had blocked our connection earlier would be gone. I hoped that it would show me he was still alive. If he was alive, we could fix everything else.

The bond thrummed faintly as I focused on it. The edges were frayed, the bright gold it had been was faded, pulsing weakly. But it was still there, and that meant Tor was too.

"He fought hard." The words were like acid, hate coating them. I turned my attention from Torren to the man speaking. He stepped from the shadows and as the light ghosted over his face, there was no denying the scorn displayed there. My heart broke at the sight.

"Why?" I asked. "Why would you do all this?"

Newt's lips curled, baring his teeth. "That's the problem with you, Laney. Always wanting to understand why. Never just doing what needs to be done. It's what makes you weak."

My hands were shaking but I refused to let him see that. "You helped raise me. You taught me. You were always there."

"I was, because I had to be. Your father needed to be reminded of who he really was. His responsibilities." Newt shook his head, as if he was still overwhelmed with disappointment. "Your mother, she made him forget."

"But he didn't stay. He went back with you. We were left without him all those years."

His laughter at my statement was cruel. "He left, not to return to who he really was. He left to save her. And you. Everything he did was for the two of you. He forgot about us. What we truly needed from him. He expected us to change like he did."

"He loved us." Despite everything that had happened, all that had gone on, I didn't doubt the truth of what I said. "He loved us. You make that sound like it's a crime."

Newt stepped across the dais to where Torren lay at the foot of the altar. He pressed the toe of his boot into Tor's side, shoving him. Torren rolled, sliding against the polished wood of the altar's base, his arm flopping at a weird angle as he collapsed onto his side. The moan he released was audible. His eyes didn't open but that sound made me hopeful.

"This is what love does," he said, pointing to Torren. "You had the chance to seize your power, to use the bond to become stronger. Instead, all you did was worry about how a human might be hurt. I showed you magic, control, strength. You chose weakness. Love. Exactly like he did."

Sadness overwhelmed me. Newt had been my family, an integral part of my very first memories. To see the hate raging through him and the way he'd wanted to hurt those who'd loved him was a dagger in my heart.

"And I see you didn't come alone."

I heard Cal's step behind me as he came into the church, Moose's nails tapping on the polished wood floor. I'd asked them to hang back while I assessed the situation. To give me some time. Apparently, my time was up.

I shrugged. "You should know this already, Newt. I'm stubborn, not stupid."

"Condemning them as well as yourself?" Newt shook his head again. Scorn coated every word he launched at me. "You'll never learn all you could've become, Laney. So trapped by sentiment."

I let the words bounce off me, as if they were arrows

hitting a shield. They didn't have the power to hurt me. But I needed to know something.

"Did you kill my mother, Newt? Were you the one who took her away from me?" I couldn't hide the pain in my voice, the way grief still made it shake. I didn't bother. He wouldn't have believed it even if I had.

"It was necessary." His answer was cold, clinical. "A means to an end. To remind your father of who he is meant to be. And to show you what you would become."

Rage boiled up under my breastbone, and this time I didn't fight to subdue it. Instead, I welcomed it, letting the hot anger flow into every part of me. "She trusted you, I know that. She believed you were her friend. She considered you part of our family."

The smile he gave me was cruel. "Which proves my point. Weakness." He stepped down off the dais, stopping when he was in front of me in the aisle. "Now, make your choice, Delaney. Weakness? Or strength?"

Chapter Forty-One

I COULDN'T TEAR my eyes away from Torren's bloodied form. He hadn't asked for any of this. He was here because of me. My thoughts flew to Cal and Moose, to the fact that they'd refused to let me face this alone. I thought of my mother, how she'd been brave enough to love Angus even when it meant she could lose everything.

I lifted my eyes to meet Newt's, the smirk and disdain on his face. He was leaning toward me, waiting for my answer.

"I choose strength." With that, I pulled my gun from its holster, raised it to the level of his chest and fired.

The blessed bullet shot forward as he flinched, shock in his eyes, like he hadn't expected me to actually take the shot. It buried itself in the muscle, directly above where his heart would be. I cursed under my breath. A little high and to the left. Like all my targets. The impact dropped him to his knees, blood dripping onto the floor. I'd wounded him, but for now, he'd live. My only hope to end this quickly had been a direct hit to the heart. Higher level demons were that much harder to kill.

I heard Cal's voice as he called his sword to life. The light from its flames lit me from behind, casting my shadow over Newt as I stood in front of him. Moose barked a warning, the short yip confirming what we'd suspected. Newt hadn't come here alone either.

Demons poured from the alcoves at the back, swarming toward us. The church was too small to hold the horde that appeared. Newt must have had a rift open. We were easily outnumbered. I ran up the three steps to where Torren still lay and checked him over quickly. His wounds were no longer bleeding freely, but he looked like he'd been chewed on.

I shifted him up, intending to pull him away from the center of the fighting. In a dark corner, he'd at least be safe, partially hidden from sight and at less risk of being accidentally hit. We'd deal with the injuries he already had when the battle was over. He groaned as I moved him, his eyes fluttering open.

"Laney," he whispered, the dried blood on his cheek cracking as he spoke. "You shouldn't have come here."

"Sorry," I said in return. I sat him up, wrapping my arms around his torso from behind and leaning backwards. He slid with me and I continued our slow progress step by step. "Not coming wasn't really an option."

"He's going to kill you."

I gritted my teeth as I hauled him back a few feet more. "He's welcome to try." I took a deep breath and pulled again, sliding him up against the wall so he could rest there. "Hells, you're heavy, man. Might have to put you on a diet when we get home."

He gave me a weak smile, one that revealed bloodstained teeth, and my stomach turned over at the thought of what he'd endured. "You start cooking dinner and I promise I'll lose weight."

I appreciated his attempt at humor. I kissed him quickly on the cheek. "Sounds like a good plan. Now, stay here. We'll be back for you."

I crept away from him, staying in the shadows and making my way deliberately to the edge of the altar. Cal was in the center of the church, pushing back the demons who'd swarmed into the chapel. Moose was fighting beside him, even in his Yorkie form, darting in between their legs, sinking his teeth into whatever vulnerable parts he could reach.

My gun came smoothly into my hand now, all the drills and practice with Cal having paid off. I sighted my first target and pulled the trigger in one smooth motion. This time my aim was true, the bullet flying straight into the back of a demon's head. We'd seen that blessed bullets could put them down. I was going to make every single one count.

I could feel the darkness working its way through me as I fought, but I refused to let it gain control this time. I funneled it into my core, using it as fuel to do what had to be done. Miss Tilly had warned me I couldn't hide from it. She was right, I knew that now. But I could use it.

A demon turned toward me, raising a clawed hand to swipe at me as its partner did the same. I shot the first one, not even watching as it fell with a shriek. I brought my gun around, but I was a hair too slow. The other demon grabbed it, tearing it from my grip and then reaching for me. I dodged back then ducked as the demon swiped at my head. My empty hand dropped with practiced ease to the inside of my boot, pulling my new knife free. I lunged up, burying the blessed blade in the demon's gut and then yanking it free. Black blood poured out from the gaping wound.

The demon collapsed at my feet and I pulled the gun from its clawed hand before I moved on to the next one. I wiped the blade as clean as I could on the side of my pants and examined it quickly. The steel shone silver in the light, no evidence of damage. "Must've been one Hell of a blessing," I muttered to myself. I'd have to ask Callum about that when this was all over.

I fought my way through the crowd, slashing with one hand and firing with the other. Moose and Cal still held a small area clear in the center, but it was shrinking. I could feel Cal's strength beginning to wane as he tired. I used the bond between us and shoved some of my energy his way. I needed him strong if we were going to make it to the end of this. His surprise echoed back to me through our connection.

He'd told me this could be a gift. I was hoping he was right.

When I saw an opening, I slid forward on my knees through the gap, my blade slicing through the Achilles tendon of a demon as I passed. Another reached out, claws snagging in my hair and whipping my head around. Cal's blade sliced through its arm before it could do me any harm.

I came to my feet in the center, next to Callum and Moose. My gun had locked open, so I ejected the spent mag and slapped a spare one in. Ready for the next round. We formed up together, the three of us, and faced our opponents. We'd done a fair bit of damage, but there were still too many willing and able to fight. I caught sight of Newt standing on the dais, a triumphant grin on his face.

I took a deep breath, preparing myself for the onslaught. "Cal, I need you to promise me, no matter what happens, you'll get to Torren and get him out of here."

I could feel his eyes on me as he shifted at my back, but I didn't look at him. "Promise me. Please."

I heard his answer, whispered as he turned away to face the next threat. "I promise."

I nodded, steeling myself for what was coming. The demons in front of me screamed and charged. I lifted my gun, aimed and as I began to pull back on the trigger, the roof came down.

Chapter Forty-Two

Cal knocked me to the floor, his body landing on top of mine as he shielded me from the stained-glass roof panels that had shattered above us. Moose's fur tickled my skin as he crowded in close, and then the shimmer of Callum's shield spell appeared, protecting us from the rain of debris that bounced down around us.

The floor shook beneath me as something heavy landed and I gasped as a roar sounded close by. Cal's breath tickled the back of my neck as he whispered to me. "Delaney, stay down. Don't move."

I gripped his fingers in response, not wanting to say anything even though I was dying to know what had happened.

"NEWTON!" The word shook what remained of the structure and Cal's weight pressed down on me even further as Moose whined in my ear. It was a voice I recognized. The Devil himself had arrived.

"Newton. Show yourself. Now!" The command was unmistakable. Even though he hadn't called my name, a part of me responded to it all the same. It was only because Cal wouldn't yield, holding me still beneath him, that I didn't stand up and reveal myself to him.

"I'm here." Newt's voice rang out, less powerful but angry. Angry and unafraid. I heard the tapping of his boots across the floor as he stepped forward.

"How dare you challenge me. I raised you up after The Fall, I gave you a place Below, and now you defy me? You try to take what's mine?"

Footsteps drew closer to where we waited behind Callum's shield. It couldn't render us invisible, but I understood why Cal didn't want to draw attention to where we were. My father and Newt could fight this battle between themselves. It might even give us an opening to rescue Torren and get him somewhere safe.

Newt's cruel laughter sounded. "Yours? It hasn't truly been yours since you gave it all up for that *woman*. I've carried it for you. Tried to calm the other demons who wanted things back to the way they used to be. I argued for you. I fought and killed for you. Even after she was gone, you still refused to return to who were you meant to be. *You failed in your duty.* But I will not. This world was meant to be ours. You promised us!"

I couldn't see them, but I could hear them shifting into position, preparing themselves for the battle to come. The image of two gunfighters squaring off in a dusty street flitted through my mind and pulled a nervous giggle from me. I swallowed the sound as much as I could, still hoping to escape notice.

There was an explosion above us and something shattered. I closed my eyes with every blast of sound, trusting that Callum's shield would hold for as long as we needed it to. I heard a grunt off to my left and the fearful pants of the few demons my father hadn't killed when he'd appeared. We weren't the only ones trying to avoid attention and leave this place alive.

Cal whispered, "When I tell you to move, I need you to roll to your right and take the shot." I nodded my head, acknowledging his instruction. The floor beneath us shook again and I heard a howl of pain. Whether that had been Newt or my father I didn't know. At this point, I wasn't sure which one was the lesser evil.

There was another bang, another pained exhalation and then my father's voice came from beside our shelter. "You build an army of your own Below, you fail to protect my wife, and then you dare to challenge me. This will not stand, Newton." His words were punctuated by the sound of something heavy being dragged across the floor.

Newt chuckled, but it sounded painful and wet, as if he was laughing around blood. "You haven't figured it out yet, have you? She made you stupid and blind to everything else. You used to be Lucifer, the one who rallied us to fight beside him. You were our leader, our morning star. We gave up everything for you. But you, you gave us up for her. I didn't fail to protect her. I killed her. To bring you back to us. But still, you refuse to see. So, I'll take it all from you. Everything, Above and Below."

There was a taut silence hanging in the church and it was Cal who broke it. "Now, Delaney. Move!"

His weight lifted clear and I rolled to the right, my gun already in my hand and coming up. I found Newt and sighted down the barrel with my left eye. I tightened my grip, holding my hands steady and pulled the trigger right as Callum dropped the shield around us.

I had the element of surprise but Newt, injured as he was, still had some of his speed. He tried to dive out of the way, and it was that shift in position that saved him. The bullet caught him in the shoulder, drawing a scream of pain from him, but it wasn't enough to end this once and for all.

"Why won't you just die!" he screamed at me, words I'd never dreamed I'd hear coming from his mouth. I flinched, the emotional blow of his hatred hitting me hard, making me hesitate. He seized the opportunity, an orb of fiery magic appearing in his hand. He threw it at me, and I froze, knowing I wasn't fast enough to avoid being hit. Without my magic, I had no way to protect myself.

My eyes found Cal, who'd taken up a position across the room, intending to flank our enemies. I could see the truth in his eyes as he realized he was too far away to save me.

Without my bracelet, he couldn't use a shield spell to deflect the magic. Time seemed to slow, giving me one last chance to think through all that had brought us to this point. So many things I was thankful for. So many things I regretted.

A shadow moved off to my left, but I didn't turn toward it. I would face my end. I would not look away.

The Devil's form suddenly appeared in front of me, intercepting the magical hit. I was stunned, paralyzed with shock. He didn't scream or cry out. I heard him gasp as he stumbled back two steps before dropping to his knees. He put a hand out to steady himself against the floor, but his arm buckled, and he collapsed. A shiver crawled across his skin, his appearance wavering, and in an instant, the Devil at my feet was gone. In his place was the man who'd raised me. He was as he'd always been, mahogany curls, his worn leather jacket and torn jeans. Pain creased his face as he looked up at me.

"Angus," I dropped to the ground beside him, my hands going to his stomach where blood was leaking through. I pressed down on it, hating the agonized sound he made in response. I needed to slow the bleeding, to buy him enough time so he could be healed. "Please, stay still. We can fix this."

"Delaney. Look at me." There was no command in his voice, no requirement that I do as he said. This was simply a request. I met his eyes and was surprised by the tears I saw in them. "I was wrong," he said. "I'm so, so sorry."

I shook my head. "It's okay. It's going to be okay." I tore my eyes away from him, searching for Cal. He was taking on the remaining demons that had aligned themselves in front of Newt and were pushing forward toward us. Moose was with him again, slipping in and out as he snapped at the legs of our enemies, still locked in his smaller canine form.

"Cal," I called out. "Please Cal, I need you." My voice didn't sound loud enough but the worry I felt was clearly transmitted to him through our connection. He spun, his sword cutting through the legs of three demons before he raced back to me.

I lifted my hands, covered in my father's blood, and Cal examined the wound. "This is bad," he said. "I need time to properly heal this."

I searched his eyes, understanding what he was telling me. There wasn't a quick fix. Cal had to survive this if we were going to heal Angus.

A yelp of pain had me spinning around. Newt stood, the bodies of his demons on the floor around him, holding my Hound in the air over his head. The smile on his face turned my stomach, the manic joy in it disturbing. He paused for a moment, as if he was drinking in my hurt and fear, then he threw Moose to the floor and kicked him toward me.

Moose slid across the distance, over the glass and other broken debris. He came to a stop at my feet and I choked back a sob. His eyes were filled with pain as I gathered him up in my arms, his breathing labored. Foam bubbled at the corner of his mouth. "I'm sorry," I whispered, holding him close so he would hear me. I kissed the back of his head and laid him carefully on the ground again.

The darkness I'd been holding in check flared inside me and I let it spill free. It filled me up, fury fueling me. Newt's laughter spurred it further and I felt a change settle over me as he said, "Poor little Laney. She just can't win."

I faced him straight on, not hiding the hate I felt for him. He'd taken too much from me. The thought flitted through my mind. *Make him pay.*

Kneeling beside my father, I gave him one quick look, letting him see the change in me. He gave me a short nod, as if he understood what I was going to do, but I could see the sadness in his eyes that were bright green once again. He braced himself as I plunged my hand into the open wound of his stomach, digging until my fingers brushed across what I'd been looking for. The burning piece of Hell my father always carried within him.

It came apart as I grabbed it, separating into smaller sections. My fingers closed tightly over the piece I'd found, I pulled my hand free from his wound. My father groaned, his eyes closing. I stood, turning to face Newt, the demon I'd always considered a part of my family.

I held my hand up, covered in the blood and gore of my father, wanting him to see exactly what was to come. His eyes widened, his mouth opening as if to say something, but I didn't wait. I shoved the piece of Hell I'd pulled from my father into my mouth and swallowed it down.

The burn of it scorched my throat, every inch of me on fire inside. Newt screamed, a garbled sound, and I heard Cal shout. When I opened my eyes, Newt was on his knees, Callum's flaming sword on the ground beside him, the fire dying down. Cal staggered, blood streaming from his head as he fought to stay on his feet.

I embraced the power that was now a part of me, intimately aware of its capacity for destruction. Devastation would come so easily. I smiled, enjoying the fear that settled across Newt's face as he saw it. "You have taken my mother away from me. My father. My home." Rage coated every word I spoke, and I didn't hold back. "You've hurt people I care about." My gaze dropped down to where Moose still lay, barely breathing, his small form quivering. "And you hurt my Hound."

I stepped toward him, the new magic I carried inside spilling out in waves, the heat pouring from me rippling the air. I stopped when I was directly in front of him and told him the truth. "But I won't let you take me as well."

I slid my knife free, the blessed metal stinging my skin, but I ignored the bite of pain. I whispered the word that appeared suddenly in my mind, and the blade caught fire, burning so hot the flames dancing along the edge were blue. Newt scrambled back, trying to put distance between us. I watched him with narrowed eyes, believing he had nowhere left to run. I wanted to drive my knife into him, up to the hilt, and cause him as much pain as he'd caused me. I wanted to take everything away from him and watch as he realized he had lost. I wanted to destroy him. The darkness within me whispered approvingly, goading me on.

My hesitation was all Newt needed. His hand cut through the air, tearing through space, and a rift appeared behind him. The flickering red light cast a bloody pall over his features. The rift was small, evidence that he was hurt, and his power was low, but his escape was there. He stumbled into it and I screamed, the knife flipping in my hand. I threw it with all the strength I had, the blade singing through the air. It caught him in the back, and he fell, the rift snapping shut before I could reach it.

And then we were alone, silence ringing out through the destroyed church.

Chapter Forty-Three

WE HAD WOUNDS to treat. Cal was able to get Angus stable enough for transport. Torren was safe where I'd left him in the corner of the dais and Cal left me alone with Angus while he went to heal Tor's injuries, at least well enough that he could walk to the portal under his own power. When we had a bit of privacy, Angus grabbed my hand.

"You need to know the truth." I froze, not daring to even twitch, wondering what confession he might have to make. What it could possibly mean. I didn't say anything in response or question him, hoping he'd continue. His next words hit hard. "You need to know the truth about your mother."

I gasped and his fingers tightened around mine, as if he was afraid I'd bolt. His breathing was still labored, still hitched with pain.

"Wanting your mother wasn't sudden, Delaney. Loving

her wasn't. Our marriage, yes, that was sudden and unexpected. You, very much so. But I lived with wanting her for a long time. Ran from it in fact."

I stared at my father, shock numbing me. He never talked like this. Not with me. Angus shook his head, trembling fingers scrubbing at his face, wiping away tears I couldn't see. "Why?" I asked, my voice a bare breath.

He choked out a pained laugh. "Fear, my sweet girl." Honesty was all he had to offer me right now. "When I met your mother, she didn't like me. Wasn't impressed by me at all." A sad smile passed across his face. "Any other woman in the world could have been mine and I had to fall in love with the one that didn't want to give me a second of her time."

He paused but I didn't say anything to break the silence, afraid to interrupt the moment. "She ignored me, so I found reasons she had to be with me, near me. All so I could wear her down. Make her want me. And when she finally did, when I'd won that battle, I realized I was terrified. For the first time in my entire existence, I was afraid. Because now I knew what love was. How much I needed it. How losing it could destroy me." His voice shook on the next words. "How loving me could destroy her."

His words were tumbling, falling over each other with a building force. The dam that had contained them before was broken now, nothing to stop the flow. "I fought it, Delaney. I pushed her away even when I saw how much it hurt her. I stayed as far away as I could. Until I couldn't anymore. Until I wasn't strong enough and gave in to what I wanted. Her. And then you."

His voice caught, stuck in his throat. He swallowed convulsively, fingers running through his hair like he was trying to comfort himself. "I was selfish. In the end, I took what I wanted. Selfish." He spat the words, like they tasted bad. "And this is the result."

I was stunned, my arms wrapped around my middle for warmth. My face was streaked with tears I didn't remember shedding. But I needed to know something. "Do you regret loving her?" I asked quietly.

He froze in place across from me, as if my words themselves had the power to hold him there until he answered. His eyes were wet, the fire I was used to seeing in them quenched for now. He stared at me, eyes moving over my face in increments of inches, my hair, every part of me as if he needed to memorize every detail. Like this could be our last time together.

His answer finally came, the words slow and aching. "No. I don't. I should, but I can't."

I nodded. That was the answer I'd already known in my heart. "She never regretted a moment with you either. And she wanted you to let this guilt go."

"How can I? Now? When she's dead because of me?" he asked, whispering the words.

The answer I had for him was simple. "Because she wanted you to." I leaned forward, dropping my lips to his forehead the same way he always kissed me. Then I whispered the truth to him again. "She wants you to."

The sound of a step behind us broke the moment and I turned to see Callum crossing the aisle to us with Moose in his arms. As he laid him on the floor beside Angus, I could see that Cal had healed some of his injuries. The pain of his wounds was still evident in his eyes, the depths of them focused on me. An echo of that pain radiated through my chest at the sight of him.

Angus released me, his hand dropping onto Moose's head. I watched as the air rippled around my Hound and Moose began to shift back into his true form, the block on his powers gone. As he transformed, his caramel brown fur changed to midnight black and his legs stretched out. The tips of his frightening fangs were visible again, and I was relieved to see his remaining injuries fade as he was flooded with his own magic once again. The blood that had coated his fur disappeared and he gave a happy sigh, whole once again. I hugged my giant Hell Hound then, burying my face in his silky fur. He stood there, letting me hang on him, my tears hidden from everyone else. And I heard his voice once again, clear and distinct. "*Family.*"

"Yes, we are. Whether she wants us to be or not." Callum was beside us now, apparently eavesdropping on the conversation. He helped me up and pulled me close. The bond between us vibrated with relief and happiness, and possibly, something more. He kissed me, a gentle press of his lips, then pulled back, his eyes searching mine. I could see the flames in the center of my pupils reflected back at me. "You're sure you won't come with us?"

I nodded, stepping back. "I need to go see someone. I'll meet you there when I'm done."

Cal dropped his gaze to where our fingers were twined together, his grip tightening. "Okay then. But if you don't show up, I'll come looking for you."

I gave him a little laugh, our connection flowing warm and free for now. "I'll keep that in mind."

He grinned in response, the silver portal opening behind him strong and stable. He gave my fingers one last squeeze and then he was gone, hefting Angus up to support him as they stepped onto the bridge together. Torren and Moose followed, and then the portal closed, the wind-blown debris settling back into place around me. I stood alone, looking at the destruction around me. I could leave it the way it was, piles of rubble to greet parishioners when the sun came up. A part of me wanted that. Devastation would be so very easy, and the darkness inside promised me I would enjoy it.

Instead, I made my way outside, to the front of the chapel, remembering what it had looked like before the battle had begun. The stained-glass images, the stories they told works of art. The arch of the beams that held up the roof. The beautiful doors that welcomed visitors. I held the image of it all firmly in my mind, adding in the details and colors, layering in the feeling of peace and serenity that had been there before our arrival. Then I released it all, into the world with a breath of power and a request. To return.

The chapel shivered, magic flowing over it. I closed my eyes, soaking in the sense of the power I'd let loose. When I opened them again, the chapel was as it had been, returned to its original glory.

I smiled, pleased to see something good and whole after what we'd endured.

Chapter Forty-Four

SHE WAS WAITING for me at the edge of Hazelwood, her hand resting lovingly on one of the ward stones that guarded the town. That kept evil out.

"Finally, Girl," she said, when I emerged from the portal that now swam with a mix of silver and red gold light. "Finally, you are on time."

I gave her a smile as she waved me forward with her free hand. I stepped toward her, stopping as the vibration of the stones increased, turning from serene and constant to an angry, pounding rhythm.

"Hush now," Miss Tilly said, tapping on the top of the stone with her knuckle. "We have things to discuss." The stone quieted at her command, but it didn't feel as welcoming to me as it once had.

"I can't come back here anymore, can I?" I was surprised at how much the realization hurt, another thing I'd lost along the way.

"For now," she said. "Nothing has to be forever, if we choose otherwise."

I looked away from her, my eyes finding the trampled ground we'd fought upon such a short time ago. Already, the scars of the battle had started to fade. By spring, the grass would fill in and wildflowers would begin to show. Soon there would be nothing left to mark what had happened here.

"I don't know if it's safe yet. Newt escaped Below. I'm sure I got him with a knife but..." I paused, a bright pain flaring in my chest as the depth of his betrayal hit me.

Miss Tilly watched me, her eyes understanding, and I couldn't fight the feeling that she was seeing everything I wanted to hide. She nodded, then patted the stone she leaned against. "We will keep ours safe. As before, so it will be."

I sighed, wishing I could hug her but that wasn't our way. "Will you tell everyone I said goodbye?"

"I will, but there are some waiting to see you. Word spreads quickly."

I was surprised to see three women step out of the shadows that draped the road leading into town. Donna Kay, her smile warm, was the first to reach me. She'd always been respectful of my wish to keep distance between myself and others, limiting physical contact when I could. But tonight, she disregarded that entirely, opening her arms wide to pull me into a tight hug. For a moment, it felt like my mother was hugging me again and I lost myself in the feeling of it. When she finally stepped back, she reached out and wiped the tears from my cheeks before doing the same for herself. "We'll see you again," she promised. "I'm still planning to get you in my salon so I have a chance to work on your beautiful hair." She waved goodbye and walked back into Hazelwood.

Miss Tilly's granddaughter Aften came to me next, presenting me with a brown paper bag. "There are some things you'll need in here. She says you'll know when."

"Thank you," I said, wondering what exactly might be inside. I hadn't been too proud of what I'd done with the last batch of goods I'd bought from The Hedgerow, using magic to force Moose and Callum to obey my commands. I'd left them behind then, determined to face danger all on my own. I'd never do that again. But knowing Miss Tilly, that had been part of the lesson I was meant to learn. I examined Aften's face, wincing as I saw the dark bruise from the punch I'd hit her with. "Um, I'm sorry about that, you know. I wasn't quite myself when I hit you."

She flushed, dropping her eyes to the ground. "Don't worry too much about it. She said it was a lesson we both had to learn."

I laughed at the idea. "What did she think you needed to learn from a punch?"

"How not to get punched," she said, giving me a grin. In that moment, she looked so much like her grandmother that I could easily see her stepping in as the leader of Hazelwood when the time came.

"How much do I owe for this?" I asked, holding up the bag.

"No charge," Miss Tilly called from her place at the stones. "A gift for today."

I thanked her, then waved goodbye as Aften walked over to join her grandmother. The last woman came forward, long dark hair sweeping down in front of her face. I'd never seen her hair loose before. It was always pulled back, a tight bun so severe I'd imagined it had to hurt. Anita handed me the box she carried. "It's pie. Apple. For your men and the dog."

That pulled a laugh from me, startling me so much I almost dropped the box. She steadied it for me. Her hands were cool as they brushed across my skin before she stepped back. I cradled the pie close, balancing the bag Aften had given me on top of it. "Thank you. They'll love it."

Miss Tilly whispered something to Aften, who nodded and waved goodbye to me. Then she and Anita walked back into Hazelwood. Once again, we were alone, the silence of a peaceful night surrounding us. I needed to say one last thing to her. I took a deep breath. "Thank you, for everything."

Miss Tilly left her place by the stones and came to where I stood. Seeing her this close, I was reminded of how small she really was and how deceiving looks could sometimes be. She placed her hands on mine, leaned in, and said, "We are always here to be found. Now go. You have a home to rebuild." She gave me one last smile and then returned to the stones.

I ducked my head, not wanting her to see the shine of tears in my eyes. I opened my portal and stepped inside, letting the place I needed to go next fill my mind. I didn't look back.

Acknowledgments

To my husband, thank you for everything you do to keep this world spinning when I'm lost in another, getting the stories out. To my boys, thank you for always making me laugh and your unshakeable belief in me. To my parents, my sister and my brother, thank you for putting up with me all these years and cheering me on. To my friends, thank you for the time you spent reading the early drafts, talking me through changes and filling in the plot holes. To my editor, thank you for loving these characters as much as I do. Finally, to every person in the Acorn Publishing Family, thank you for making this dream come true.

About the Author

K.A. Fox is a proud military brat who has lived all over the world but now calls the Midwest home. She uses her psychological training to facilitate successful negotiations at work and to convince her husband and three sons that she's always right. When not writing, she can usually be found hiding somewhere with a book and a bit of chocolate or chasing after her own adorable Hell Hound. Connect with her at www.imkafox.com and on Facebook at www.facebook.com/imkafox.

www.ingramcontent.com/pod-product-compliance
Ingram Content Group UK Ltd.
Pitfield, Milton Keynes, MK11 3LW, UK
UKHW041227200426
11947UKWH00034B/171